THE INTERN AND THE PLASTIC SURGEON

Sacred Heart Children's
Hospital, Book 2

Liza Collins

CONTENTS

Sacred Heart Children's Hospital
Hampstead
London Borough of Camden

Plastic and Reconstructive Surgery department

CHAPTER ONE

Jennifer

Finally, finally, I found the right department.

My first day working on plastics; a fine time to get lost. Tucked away in a basement wing, the re-constructive surgery department was hardly conspicuous. In the few years I'd been interning at Sacred Heart Children's Hospital, I'd never so much as set foot on the ward – and here I was, lost and, worse, *late* – to meet the man who was supposed to become my mentor: Mr Wesley Brookes.

Known for being a cranky bastard, I wasn't looking forward to explaining myself to him. After finding the only lift down here to be out of order, I ran breathlessly down two flights of stairs to arrive panting in the foyer, fumbling for my lanyard.

"Come on, Jen, get it together you daft cow,"

I hissed at myself, locating my lanyard only to drop my induction materials and staff handbook. They fell about my feet in an ungraceful fluttering of papers.

"Urgh!" I groaned, bending to gather them up in my arms like a newborn baby. I froze in my crouched position as the doors to the ward opened inward, revealing a pair of shoes wrapped in blue disposable covers. I clutched the papers to my chest as I let my eyes wander upward. They followed a strong pair of legs, calf and thigh muscles just discernible as they bulged in key places from inside loose scrub pants. My eyes trailed further still to a man whose expression almost made me gasp out-loud.

Two piercing bottle-green eyes were fixed on me, staring incredulously beneath endearingly full eyelashes and a hard, knitted brow. A face mask bridged a regal, aquiline nose and wrapped around the face concealed behind it. The mask was hiding what could only be a snarl. Locks of dirty-blonde hair peaked from beneath his surgical cap, curling at the nape of his neck. I recognised him instantly from his profile on the staff system.

"Dr B-Brookes," I said, stuttering as I caught my breath and came to my senses. "It's a pleasure to meet you."

I clutched the papers to my breast and held out my right hand for him to shake. His sparkling green eyes narrowed on my hand, as if looking at a specimen for dissection. After he left me hanging there for what felt like an age, his own large hand appeared and wrapped around mine, squeezing it firmly. With a sudden jolt, he pulled me to my feet, making me squeal.

"I prefer to meet my interns on their feet, if you don't mind," came his deep, silky voice from behind the surgical mask. "You are my new intern, aren't you?"

"Y-yes, sir, I am. I'm afraid the lift was broken. I had to take the stairs – "

"Spare me the feeble excuses," said Dr Brookes, his eyes narrowing on me once more.

He gave me the sensation that I was a bug under a microscope, and he, a sadistic six year old boy. At any moment, he might incinerate me in the glare of a carefully-angled magnifying glass or squash me under his thumb. A chill crept over the surface of my skin, making me shiver, and a familiar yet long-forgotten anxiety roiled in my core. I had to wonder how such a brutal glance could both excite and terrify me so – but there was no time for that right now.

"You're right, sir – it's my error. I should have left enough time. I had so much to deal with on the neonatal unit – years of just, well, crap in my locker, as well as all the loose ends I had to tie up with admin and HR and the nursing team – "

Once I found myself rambling, I simply

couldn't stop, even though I knew I was making a fool of myself. The truth was that I was terrified of meeting Wes Brookes, whose reputation preceded him as being cold and positively ruthless with his interns. The worse I felt, the more I talked – the more I talked, the more I wished I could slam my own head inside my department handbook.

"And now we're making even more excuses. Dear, oh dear," said Dr Brookes. "Do you think I find you entertaining, Dr Hurst?"

I blinked, tucking a long strand of hair behind my ear. "No, not at all, sir," I said.

"Then do you think we could keep the waffling to a minimum?"

"Absolutely," I said, nodding a little too eagerly. "No more waffling."

"Good," said Dr Brookes. "Because while Mr Hartcliffe might have found your tardiness amusing, I don't – and I certainly don't put up with nonsense excuses."

"If it's any consolation, Max – I mean, Dr Hartcliffe – hated my rambling and my lateness as well," I said. "He just got used to me – my ways, that is – eventually. Sort of."

Dr Brookes cocked a blonde eyebrow.

"Max," he said. "I haven't seen him in a while. Married, now, isn't he?"

I swallowed, feeling awkward; answering

intimate questions about my former boss while hovering in the doorway of the plastics unit seemed wrong somehow. Yet Dr Brookes asked as if he was inquiring about the weather outside, having spent too long locked away down in his bat-cave of a department.

"Yes, actually – with two children already," I said. "It's a really sweet story – "

"He's an idiot," said Dr Brookes, cutting me off mid-sentence. His tone was flat, cynical. "You can tell him I said so."

I blinked, startled, unsure how to answer. Without waiting for any response, Dr Brookes held open the door and stepped aside, ushering me in with a quick sweep of his hand.

"Come along, then," he said in a strained tone of voice, making it clear I'd wasted enough of his time.

I straightened my shoulders and met his deep green eyes as I shimmied between him and the door, ready to give him a piece of my mind if I needed to. All right, I was his intern – but I was no fledgling doctor straight out of medical school. I had a few years under my belt now, and felt I deserved a little more than to be treated like a complete rookie.

Dr Brookes wouldn't meet my gaze, his own eyes dipping and fixing on a piece of tile on the floor as I moved past him. His frown deepened, though; the wrinkle on his forehead bulging, and I thought I heard him swallow, hard, as if digesting something unpalatable.

I was rattling him already. No, not rattling – *annoying* him.

The space was much tighter than either of us had realised. As I squeezed through, my chest brushed uncomfortably against his abdomen. I realised with a startled flip of my heart that he had a hard body beneath those scrubs; smooth and formed like marble. For a cranky bastard who had to be in his mid-forties, he was hiding one hell of a body. As our torsos briefly touched, Dr Brookes pulled away quite abruptly and strode ahead down the hall, as if struck by an electric shock.

I hurried after him, conscious of the bust I hid beneath my shirt and sleeveless jumper, at least making an attempt at modesty. It was a tedious-but-necessary requirement of the dress code to hide what I knew was a voluptuous figure. One that could be a bit of a distraction on the geriatric wards, and had made for some deeply disturbing shifts in my earlier days as an intern. My mother, a surgeon and absolute battle-axe, had read me the riot act about concealing my figure long before I'd ever been accepted onto the medicine pathway at university.

Well, so much for that. I might as well have walked in wearing a bustier if I was going to brush myself against his pecs like that. But hell – Dr

Brookes was ripped. Who could have guessed that?

As I hurried down the blue-lino hall after him, I felt like I'd discovered my own little piece of treasure. It brought a smirk to my face. Come to think of it – now that I was in the mood for noticing – Dr Brookes was hiding an impressive, taut bum behind those blue scrubs, too. As he walked with his fists clenched by his sides, I noticed the tell-tale thickness of the veins snaking down his forearms, indicating he worked out a lot to maintain that body of his.

Blimey, I thought to myself, *working out was supposed to release endorphins. How much would it take to make ol' grumpy-chops smile?*

We slowed by the nurses' station, where the charge nurse was busying herself with the handover sheets for the oncoming shift. In one fluid motion she passed Dr Brookes a clipboard with the day's rota and a steaming cup of tea in a stylish white china mug, propping it up on the station worktop before him. Neither even looked at one another, and yet Dr Brookes took the clipboard and mug handle in each respective hand as if he fully expected them to be there. The nurse had inky-black hair piled up in a claw-grip and expertly refined eyebrows to match her lashes. She was already scribbling the day's surgeries up on the whiteboard as Dr Brookes took a sip of his tea. The pair of them appeared to be enacting a well-practised routine, putting them both at ease with its familiarity.

"This is Janine," Dr Brookes said between sips, his intense eyes scanning the chart he held. "She's my partner-in-crime, ensuring everything on this ward and the OR goes smoothly. Say hello, Janine," said Dr Brookes.

"Hello, Janine," she said, without so much as glancing my way.

I shook my head briefly as I watched her scribbling, deciding I would not be letting either of them get to me. There was a clear comradery going on between them that I would otherwise not be privy to. With a sigh, I relinquished my fears about not fitting in, determined not to start another internship in fear. I was here to do my job, learn about craniofacial surgery and plastics, and discover if I belonged here for *myself*. I certainly wouldn't be letting any mean surgeons or his partner-in-crime charge nurse decide for me – and not on my first morning.

"Good to meet you," I said, extending my hand over the top of the nurses' bench. I cleared my throat, making Janine pause in her scribbling. She held the black felt pen aloft as if she'd heard a mouse scrabbling about in the ceiling, and was trying to decide if she'd imagined it or not.

I cleared my throat again, a little louder this time.

In my periphery, I saw Dr Brookes glance

up from his papers. Holding firm, I kept my arm outstretched. Back when I was working with Dr Hartcliffe on the neonatal ward, fresh to the surgical intern programme, I might have missed this opportunity – out of shyness or subordination. Now, I would do no such thing. I'd promised myself I'd state my business and make myself known, and I intended to do just that. I would start as I meant to go on.

Janine slowly turned and tilted her head to one side as if not quite recognising my hand as human.

"Good to meet you," I said again, forcing Janine to look me in the eyes. They were onyx-black like her hair, and penetrating. She managed a weak smile as she took my hand, her fingers limp as they barely closed around me.

"You too," she said, pulling her hand away again. She returned to the board, jotting up the patient list.

Still, I felt I'd won something. I pulled back my arm and let it fall by my side. Dr Brookes placed the clipboard back on the nurses' station and gulped down the remainder of his still-steaming tea.

"Well," he said. "I'm glad you two could become acquainted. You'll meet the rest of the team as we go on – how familiar are you with the ward?"

"Not familiar at all," I said honestly. "This is my first introduction. Being in the thick of it on the neonatal unit – "

I thought I heard Janine give a little snort, interrupting my flow as I looked at her, puzzled.

"You haven't watched any of the induction videos online? You haven't seen the layout of the ward? Nothing?" Wes cocked his head to one side as if in disbelief that I could be so thoughtless.

I paused, remembering that we had been given some homework to watch the induction videos – but I'd been too shattered from my ongoing work with the neonates to get around to it. Besides, I preferred doing things on the fly – relying on my instincts and keeping my knowledge recall tip-top. I suspected that was an approach of mine that Dr Brookes would most definitely not be a fan of.

When he flared his nostrils in disgust at my response, I had my answer.

"I'm afraid not," I said.

"Typical bloody intern of Hartcliffe's. Late and unprepared – how very rock 'n' roll of him." Dr Brookes rolled his eyes so far I could see the gleaming whites of them. "You'll soon find that we expect a little bit more of our staff members in plastics, Dr Hurst."

"I can see that," I said, glancing briefly at Janine. I thought I saw her hand pause just briefly, as if jolted out of her rhythm by my pithy remark.

"I'll now have to waste my time showing you around the place when I should be preparing to meet with our first patient," he said, with a grunt.

The ward was coming alive around us, with the nursing and assistant teams doing the morning observations in the patient rooms running along the corridor. I could see they were busy and stretched to capacity, with bed spaces at a premium. He really would need to get started if he was to keep on schedule for the day.

"Perhaps Janine wouldn't mind giving me a quick tour?" I prompted – and again, her pen froze in mid-motion.

Dr Brookes raised his eyebrows, as if it struck him that it wasn't such a bad idea at all. As he glanced toward Janine, I wondered why he'd kept his mask on over his mouth. Did he have a cold he was trying to avoid passing on?

"Janine, do you think you'd have time to show Dr Hurst around?"

I noticed, too, that there was a sibilance to his speech – the slightest ghost of an impediment that he'd long since overcame, leaving only a gentle *hissing* on *think* and *Hurst*, where his tongue met his teeth. I couldn't be certain of that, and wondered if it wasn't just the effect of the mask. With the deep timbre of his voice, I had to admit privately that it made for a sexy mode of speech

– formal, velvety, stern, but with a slight catch. An imperfection that only served to highlight the beauty of its surroundings.

Janine popped the pen lid back on her marker and turned to face me with such a flat expression that I almost laughed out loud. She was absolutely *not* in the mood for me. Never mind, I thought – *I'll win her around.* I'd win them all around. They'd see.

"It'd be my pleasure," she said in a strained voice that fooled nobody, and apparently didn't intend to. "I've a heap of admin to be getting on with before I even take a temperature this morning, but apparently that can all wait."

"Thanks, Janine. I owe you one," said Dr Brookes. "Dr Hurst – meet me in my office in half an hour. Do not be late, or I'll deny you entry."

"No problem," I said, stepping backwards as Janine rounded the station.

She was short and plump, but her body was hour-glass and all-woman, her skin a cool mocha that worked well with her deep red lipstick – an interesting choice for work in a hospital, although she was the charge nurse. Maybe she considered it to be her war paint.

"You owe me a lot more than one, Dr Brookes," she said, curling a finger at me, indicating that I was to follow her. I wondered what on earth she could mean by that; they were talking in a secret language, the kind that develops after working together for years. I found myself envying it, wishing I could have put roots down like that; wondering if I should have remained in the neonatal unit after all.

Dr Brookes gave a sniff – the briefest threat of a laugh – before his stern expression returned. He twirled his empty mug by the handle, looping it around on his finger, before striding away down the corridor. He was tall as well as built, I realised, watching him go. I looked again at the locks of cherubic blonde hair at the nape of his neck, curling where they met the collar of his scrubs. It was a welcome contrast to his otherwise severe and impatient demeanour.

"Can I tear your eyes away for a moment, Dr Hurst? There's a lot I need to show you and practically no time at all in which to do it," said Janine, her eyes narrowing on me as my gaze left Dr Brookes and fell on her.

"Of course," I said, realising my heart was beating fast. What the hell was going on with me? "Let's crack on, absolutely. You have my full attention."

"Lucky me," I heard Janine mutter under her breath as she led the way.

CHAPTER TWO

Wesley

Why me? It was all I could think as I whipped off my surgical mask and tossed it aside on my desk. The cup I twirled irritably by the handle was chucked down similarly. Why give me a busty blonde intern with a will of steel and a happy-go-lucky aura about her?

Why sacrifice the poor lamb to a miserable sod like me, who would only drag her spirits down to match mine?

It had been many, many years since I'd felt so self-conscious around another colleague – certainly never an intern. If it wasn't my general awkwardness I was conscious of, it was my speech. Soon enough she would see my defect and know instantly why I wanted to become a plastic surgeon. She'd give me that pitying look that so many women gave me – certainly more than enough women when my mother was young, and

I was a little boy in shorts – and I would feel like a child again, ashamed of his face.

Well, I was still Wes Brookes; still skilled, celebrated around he globe, called out for complicated cases where I could really shine and make a difference. I didn't usually worry about what anybody thought of me – that was all in the past. Why, then, did one brief meeting with Jennifer Hurst make me feel like a schoolboy again, hiding behind my PPE?

I flexed my fingers, feeling agitated; my veins were popping as the blood rushed through them. If I didn't have such a packed morning ahead of me, I'd be tempted to burn off some of my agitation in the on-site gym. I was feeling antsy, pent-up...and what the hell was going on inside my briefs? An image entered my mind; a split second when Jennifer shuffled between me and the door frame and I felt her soft bosom brush by me, followed by the scent of shampoo from her long golden hair.

Instinctively I had wanted to reach out and slide my hands around her waist, pull her in, and nuzzle my face into her neck where I could breathe in more of her. Just one whiff of her was enough to leave me entranced, to the point where I had been forced to whip myself away and pull myself out of it. She was a heady perfume who had left me feeling intoxicated.

"Get your head in the game, you silly

bastard," I told myself, sifting through the papers on my desk. The words and names blended together as Jennifer's heady scent came alive in my mind once more.

Another image entered my head; the way her honest, pale-blue eyes met mine, with kindness shining in them. It was a kindness I wanted to put my faith in, but never would. Trust wasn't something that developed easily for me; it would take years to believe what I saw in that one perfect glance.

Knowing me, I would keep my intern at arm's length and she would be doomed to confusion, wondering if she was the problem.

I collapsed in my desk chair and sighed, lifting my arms behind my head and resting back on them. There was, of course, another issue – she bore the slightest resemblance to Rebecca, my ex-fiancé. The girl my parents had adored; the one who devastated them when I returned home to Surrey, a broken young man.

Sometimes I found myself wondering if she and Theo, my best friend, were still happy together. I'd heard through the grapevine that they were married now, living the life I'd planned with her. I had abstained from looking them up online, sparing my mental health. To be attracted to Jennifer for the physical qualities I'd seen in my ex was more than mind-boggling. Jennifer was more than Rebecca; I could see that already. Rambling, absent-minded, yes – but assured, assertive. Eager. There was a spark within her that could be seen instantly, lighting up her kind and welcoming eyes.

Still, their physical similarities were a very cruel reminder of my ex's betrayal, and an even worse reminder of something I'd been putting out of my mind for weeks now.

My parents – well-meaning darlings that they were – were visiting the city in a month's time, and I'd have to answer more brutal, desperate questions about my love life. *Why aren't you married yet, darling? Haven't you met someone special?*

You can't pine after Rebecca forever, dear boy.

I didn't. I was over Rebecca. But I wasn't over my total *lack* of Rebecca. The fact was I never planned to fill the space she left; not with another woman, not ever. I'd been burned once and I was never going back for more. My work had replaced her, and I was reaping the rewards of that.

I would have to re-frame Jennifer in my mind somehow. I'd have to block out her long, luscious golden hair, her womanly figure, the sweet freckles on her nose –

The phone on my desk blared. I frowned, glancing up at the old analogue clock on the wall above my desk. Half an hour had gone by! An entire thirty minutes wasted on my emotions. I was due to meet my first patient for the day, and Janine hadn't brought Jennifer back yet.

I groaned, picking up the phone to the surgical suite – it would be the booking nurse in charge of admissions, wondering where the hell I was.

"I'll be right with you," I said, scooping up my notes – I would have to read them on the walk round. "Just running a little late with my intern."

Storming from my office, I allowed an anger to build up inside me that would be disproportionate to the crime committed, and I jolly-well knew that. But I had been pretty bloody clear, hadn't I? I'd told her not to be late again, and *again*, she'd left me hanging. At this rate she'd be sacked from my programme before the day was out.

The staff nurses and HCAs parted before me as I bowled angrily through the ward, making my way to the crafting and prosthetics rooms in the north wing. I knew they had to be there if they followed the natural layout of the place. I ignored the nervous faces of my staff, knowing they could feel my seething anger; knowing they were afraid of me. I wasn't proud of it, but as the adrenaline pumped through me, I found a new energy putting a spring in my step. *Sod the lot of them*, I thought – they all knew the score. *You don't piss off Dr Brookes*.

I burst into the crafting room, eliciting a startled jump from the three women occupying the room. There was Janine, looking instantly apologetic as she raised her hands in surrender.

"I couldn't pry her away," said Janine, shaking her head. "I *told* her we were late –"

"It's my fault Dr Brookes, honestly – she was so interested in my work that I couldn't help showing off." Claire, our sculptor-in-chief, looked pleadingly at me as she gestured toward the works of art scattered about the work station.

Jennifer was seated, calmly turning a sculpture between her hands, the way a jeweller would hold a diamond up to the light to examine the refractions within it. It was a beautifully crafted eye piece for one of our patients; a teenage girl who had lost an eye to the removal of a malignant tumour. Thanks to Claire, we would replace the missing eye and surrounding tissues and structure with a perfectly proportioned mould. It would blend in with her face and, at a glance, appear like an unblemished part of her.

All my energy fell off a cliff as I observed Jennifer's concentration. She looked to be absolutely fascinated by the eye piece, giving it her full and undivided attention.

I was taken aback by the clear respect she had for Claire's work. Here I was, about to admonish her for her distinct *lack* of respect for me...and now I found myself speechless.

Claire, I realised, was still stuttering away with her excuses. I held up a hand to gently silence her. Jennifer, sensing the change in atmosphere, finally glanced over her shoulder at me. As her gaze met mine, my heart sank – there it was, the moment I was dreading. I realised too late that I wasn't wearing my mask, and the reaction she gave me would be honest and unfiltered.

She let out a weak scream, flinching as she did so – the eye piece dropping out of her hand.

Janine, quick as a dart, snatched the eye piece mid-air before it hit the hard white desk. Claire, cupping her hand over her mouth, let out an audible sigh of relief.

As I spoke, I was careful not to betray my inner feelings about her reaction. It wouldn't be the first time a woman had responded to me like that, after all.

"I told you not to be late," I said firmly. "I specifically told you not to be late."

Jennifer stood up abruptly, her eyes fixed on me. The cool, icy blue pools of her eyes made me shiver; I couldn't hold her gaze. I let my own eyes fall away from her, fixing on the desk and the precise sculptures that Claire had spent weeks and months producing. What was that awful feeling that crept over me like an unwelcome fever?

Was it shame?

"I'm s-s-sorry, Dr Brookes," said Jennifer. I could feel her brutal studying of me like a burn searing my skin. I wanted to ask her to look away, to not stare at me like that – but I wouldn't. *This is who I am. To hell with it.*

"I got so excited about the sculptures. I guess I just got carried away."

I relaxed a little, the stiffness in my shoulders softening. She was excited about our work here – well, that I could understand. It was nice, even, for a colleague to appreciate the near-miracles we performed on our ward. Claire was an artist, pure and simple, and she made our work possible with her skills. She gave our patients hope that they could continue their lives with some sense of normality after the trauma of losing a very real part of themselves.

I understood very well what it was like to be stared at; to be a curiosity for others. This way, we could at least give them a face to be proud of after the cancer was dealt with.

"We'll have to walk and talk," I said, summoning Jennifer with a gesture of my hand. She obeyed, smoothing down her jumper as she got up from her seat. I turned and walked out of the room, trusting that she would follow me. I was afraid that I would linger on her body in that jumper far too long, doing myself no favours whatsoever.

"Dr Brookes, I'm so sorry – " Jennifer began as we walked briskly down the hall. I passed her the papers with our patient's information – including photographs of the affected areas of his jaw – and silenced her.

"Wow," was all she could say, examining the papers. "Poor kid,"

"Our tests indicate that it's actually a benign tumour, part of a genetic mutation of his tumour suppressing genes. Unbeknownst to him, he has a propensity for these tumours – though until now he'd never had one bigger than the size of a pea." I led us out of the ward and across the way to the surgical suites. "One morning, he woke up for school and found his jaw was locked together, and an agonizing pain was searing through every nerve in his head and neck."

"Where exactly is the tumour? In the bone?" asked Jennifer.

"Some of it is," I said, using my lanyard to gain access to the ward. "It's a pesky, sticky thing – attaching itself to all sorts. Soft tissues, bone, nerves. We'll have to spend some time with him and properly assess the situation over several stages when we operate. He's booked into the OR at 11.00 a.m. this morning."

"We're meeting him now?"

"We're meeting him now."

"And I'll be scrubbing in?"

"You'll be scrubbing in," I said, pausing in the hall with my hand raised. Jennifer stopped abruptly, the breath catching in her throat. Saying what I was about to say wouldn't be pleasant, but I fell it necessary.

"But if you respond to that young lad's face," I began in a hushed whisper, "the way you responded to mine – then I'll see to it you don't meet any more of my patients, and you'll be off the programme."

A deep frown came over Jennifer's innocent, fresh face.

"Hey – "

The urgency in Jennifer's voice – in fact, the hurt that I detected – caught my attention. I folded my arms over my chest, looking down at her as she battled whatever thoughts were racing through her mind. She looked as if she had too many things to say, and no idea where to begin. Eventually she found the words.

"I may be many things, Dr Brookes. Late, for one. Sometimes distracted, especially if something interesting catches my attention. But what I will never be is rude," said Jennifer.

Anger swelled inside me, but I kept it at bay – it was a demon I was very familiar with. Like a grumbling dog by my side, I patted its head and let it return to its sleeping position at my feet.

"I beg to differ," I said in a clipped tone.

Her eyes flitted about my face, lingering on my lips, my nose, on the jagged sewn-together appearance of the cleft between my lip and nostril. I saw how they followed the line of my scar up beside my nose, finishing in the nook of my eye socket. I forced myself to withstand the discomfort, letting her take me in like an odd specimen.

"When I screamed," she said steadily, "I did so because I was surprised at the interruption. I did *not* scream because of you."

I found myself flinching and realised that her hand was on my arm, as if to reassure me. Without even thinking, I shrugged it off. I bristled at her touch, the anger overwhelming me. Old, long-abandoned habits returned. I wanted to call her a liar; to ask her to admit that my face disturbed her, like I would have when I was a teenager. Wasn't she bold enough to tell me? But I didn't – I wouldn't. It would be unprofessional and, in any case, I wouldn't give her the satisfaction.

Instead, I smirked.

"Spare me the gentle encouragement, Dr Hurst," I said, snatching the papers from her grasp. "If my face frightens you, then you'll find my temper unbearable."

I expected her to drop it, taking the out I had provided her with – but she didn't. She seemed to see through the sardonic exterior that I relied on to convince people I was above the nonsense of any judgements surrounding my appearance.

Once again, Jennifer Hurst was surprising me.

"I did not scream about your face," she said firmly.

I cocked an eyebrow. "You don't think I'm an ogre, then? A monster?" I smiled cruelly, shaking my head. Jennifer held firm, betraying nothing. Could it be that she was being sincere?

"You're incredibly handsome, Dr Brookes," she said softly. A blush crept up her neck and flooded her face, showing me in an instant that she was being genuine. I found myself swallowing hard, my mouth completely dry.

"You could actually drive me to distraction." Jennifer forced her gaze away from me, looking toward the far end of the corridor where we should be headed. "But I intend to be professional regardless of that. Can you do the same?"

"What's that supposed to mean?" I croaked, wondering why my throat was suddenly like the Sahara desert.

"Well – are we going to spend all morning talking about you and your face, or are we going to focus on our patients?"

Now I felt myself blushing, and I resented it. She was implying that I was being self-centred, almost...vain, in talking about myself. I supposed in a roundabout way, she was right.

"*Our* patients?" I asked, cocking an eyebrow once more.

Jennifer held her head high. "Our patients, Dr Brookes. I'm a member of your team now. You need to trust me, and I need to trust you."

I paused, taking her words in. She was right. She was absolutely right. I allowed myself the briefest smile, so fleeting that she might have missed it.

"Call me Wes," I said flatly. Jennifer blinked rapidly, seemingly in surprise. I turned and led the way to the assessment room where my – no, *our* – patient would be waiting. *Incredibly handsome? Driving her to distraction?*

Had I dreamed that she had uttered those words out loud?

Either way, her honesty and integrity had blown everything else out of the water – even the unsettling warm sensation I'd felt when she described the patient as ours, something we shared together. I was almost dizzied by it. She had passed some sort of test that I hadn't realised I'd set for her, and I was glad of it. But the real test, in terms of her career, would begin now.

And I was very keen, indeed, to see how she fared there.

CHAPTER THREE

Jennifer

As Dr Brookes – I mean, Wes. Wesley? Wes? Oh gosh, that would take some getting used to – led us into the small clinical room to meet our patient, I took slow, deep breaths. I wasn't so much nervous about meeting Eric, our fifteen-year-old patient, but more about keeping my bearings after *that* conversation.

What in the world had I been thinking, letting him know that I was attracted to him like that? On my first day, too. Talk about a complete and utter lack of professionalism. I smiled briefly at Eric and his mother as I shook their hands, knowing I would probably not be here tomorrow. I almost wanted to apologise to them in advance of their disappointment. It was never a good thing to begin a case with one doctor and finish with another – the continuity was so important for the patients and their families.

Well, I may have messed up – although he had softened, and asked me to call him Wes – but I would be sure to do a damn good job while I was here. I would observe, I would listen, I would reassure – and most of all, I'd let Wes lead and do what he did best.

Seeing him in action was certainly something I was looking forward to.

Wes took a seat on a rolling stool and rested his arms on his knees.

"Good to see you, Eric. You've met Dr Hurst – Jennifer – who will be assisting me this morning during your surgery."

Eric smiled sheepishly. He was a handsome lad; tall, bronzed, with dark hair – he looked like he'd be a popular, sporty kid in school. The left side of his face, particularly around the area where his mouth met his cheek and jaw, seemed off, giving him a lopsided smile. His mother, who had his dark hair and skin, looked close to tears already. I understood. Seeing her child reduced in confidence, with a concealed tumour changing his face, had to be difficult.

Something about finally being in the assessment room often brought hidden emotions to the surface like that.

"Now, I'm going to remind you and mum of what it is we're actually going to be doing today, and you'll have the chance to ask any questions you have for me," said Wes.

He span his stool around and faced the computer, typing quickly. He logged in and brought up the 3d imaging of Eric's face; a white three-dimensional model of his skull filled the screen, turning as Wes worked the direction pads on the keyboard. An area the size of a clenched fist was highlighted in pink around the left side of the mandible, covering half the maxilla and a portion of his zygomatic bone. About a quarter of his face had been invaded by the benign tumour.

Although Eric mercifully did not have cancer to contend with, he was at risk of it spreading and causing irreparable damage to the nerves in his face and neck. If the tumour wasn't removed, he would suffer, and the tumour could likely spread to other inoperable areas.

Being as it was so close to his eyes and brain stem, I was glad he'd found out about the tumour when he had.

"These are the portions of bone that we will be excising this morning. Once we've dealt with this and received our lab results to determine exactly what we're dealing with, we can see about keeping any more tumours from appearing," said Wes, keeping his voice steady and matter-of-fact.

I noticed, however, that there was a softness to his voice that I hadn't heard before now – something he saved, maybe, for his patients. A tenderness that he felt only his patients were worthy of.

"During the excision, we'll be replacing parts of your skull with bone and muscle taken from your hip. Grafting it will be quite tricky, because it'll take a great deal of time and precision, so you'll be under for a good six hours or so – potentially more," said Wes.

Eric's mother held his hand and squeezed it, glancing at him nervously.

"We'll be using state of the art technology to graft those pieces of bone and bolt them together with a flexible mechanism that'll enable you to speak, to eat, you name it," said Wes, unable to help himself from smiling.

I found myself smiling, too. It was very good news for Eric – apart from some slight scarring, he should have a fully-functioning jaw after the tumour was removed.

Wes' face was chiselled, undeniably handsome – and somehow I found the deep line that ran from his upper lip, under his nose and around to his eye socket wholly attractive. I longed to ask him how it had come about, and what condition he had been born with, but I knew that would be rude. Surgeries would not have been as advanced as they are now, back when he was a child. With today's medicine and surgical techniques, that scar would be practically invisible.

His speech was definitely affected, but it gave his voice a sort of rasping that made the hairs on my arms stand on end, and gave me shivers. Even Eric's mother seemed beguiled by him despite her fear, unable to tear her gaze away from his dazzling green eyes.

"We can go over that in more detail if you like, and I can show you some of the bolts and mechanisms we'll be using. For now, do you have any questions for me?"

Eric licked his lips, which seemed dry and parched – potentially his salivary glands were affected by the tumour.

"Will I look like you once it's over?"

"Eric!" his mother cried, batting him on the arm.

I held my breath, glancing uneasily at Wes. Knowing, now, that he had some sensitivities about his appearance sent a little bolt of terror through me when Eric asked that question.

But I needn't have worried.

"What?" asked Eric, glancing back at his mother. "I want to know."

Wes only smiled, cocking an eyebrow as he shook his head. "No, Eric. You won't look like me. My type of scarring is rarely seen nowadays, with technologies far more advanced than they were when I was small."

Eric looked relieved, and I knew that had to have stung Wes – but he didn't look shaken, not even a bit. In fact, his expression was one of fatherly understanding. I realised, then, that he understood Eric because he had once been Eric's age – scared, with an affected face, knowing that he would have to face society and all the questioning glances his face would bring.

Eric was likely already suffering this, with his half-paralysed smile very clear on his otherwise handsome young face.

"Did you have what I have?" asked Eric, his voice sounding meek and – what was that I detected? – a hopeful tone in the upwards inflection of his voice.

"I was born with my condition," said Wes, clasping his strong hands together and wringing them. With his elbows resting on his knees, he looked more like a school football coach than a doctor, advising one of his young players.

"Back then, I would have been described as having a monstrous defect. I was well into my childhood before they could fix me up completely. One of my classmates once found a photograph of a hammer-headed bat and taunted me, calling me bat-face because of the way my defect came all the way up under here."

Wes pointed to the area under his eye where

the deep line finished.

"My issue was rare and not particularly understood. It affected my breathing, my sense of smell, all sorts. I suffered terrible congestion as a baby, giving my parents the fright of their lives whenever I caught a cold. You might find that your family become a little bit precious about you." Wes glanced at Eric's mother, who welled up with tears – he clearly wasn't wrong about that one.

"But it's only because they're keen to get this out of the way so you can go on and live your life, which is what we're going to do this morning. You needn't worry about any comments on your face, Eric. You'll look good as new– and not a bit like me."

I wondered if Dr Brookes realised just how much any young boy would want to grow up to look like him. It stung to hear that he'd been taunted as a child, before his facial condition had been properly amended, but he had grown into exactly what I'd described to him – incredibly handsome, deep scar and all.

"I wouldn't mind a sick scar like that," said Eric, half-grinning. He flinched, holding a hand to his jaw – no doubt the nerve pain was giving him some grief.

Dr Brookes raised his eyebrows as if surprised to hear that, but he smiled all the same. His teeth were straight and white, his smile charming in a chiselled, square jaw. I found myself longing to pull off his surgical cap and let loose his hair, and see if it matched the rest of him in its beauty.

I wondered if Wes even saw himself at all, or if he still looked in the mirror and saw the little boy with the face like a bat – feeling unfinished, not good enough. It would certainly explain his defensive, sometimes outright hostile attitude.

"Well, if you've no more questions then we'll get you to the pre-op room and start preparing. Don't worry, you'll be in excellent hands – Janine will help you get settled in. She's prepared thousands of my surgeries over many, many years – I simply couldn't live without her," said Wes, standing up and shaking Eric's hand again.

I felt a little pang of jealousy to hear how much he valued Janine – Janine, who had been frosty as we took our tour to say the least, and who apparently didn't see much value in me. I began to wonder if there wasn't something going on between the two of them. Maybe he had a thing for brunettes with deep, dark eyes and moody faces.

"I'll see you in there, Eric," I said, shaking his hand and then his mother's. I was pumped for the surgery. This would be my first bone graft, and I was positively buzzing now that we were almost ready to begin.

♥

As we scrubbed in and the rest of the surgical team busied themselves around Eric, who was relaxed and sedated now, I thought about the taunting Wes had talked about.

"That was kind of you, Dr Brookes – I mean, Wes – what you told him about yourself," I said. "Now he won't feel alone about it all."

Wes scrubbed up and down his strong forearms, smoothing down the strands of hair under a soapy lather. He shrugged. "Eric will be just fine. He's a good-looking lad – we'll leave him with beautiful skin, not a scratch on him. You'll see. That is, after the sutures have healed. He's in for a bit of a shock when the painkillers wear off, too."

"No doubt," I said, rinsing my hands and arms thoroughly. "I, er – did a little search on my phone just before we came to theatre. A hammerhead bat, huh? Yikes."

Wes' deep-thinking face, which seemed permanently set in a frown, suddenly brightened as he tossed his head back in laughter. His shoulders shook as he chuckled, making me laugh too, to the point where I barely registered my surprise at seeing him appear so happy.

"Ugly bastards, aren't they?"

"You're telling me. There's no way you looked like one of those," I said – tempted to add that whatever bat resembled him was one lucky little sod.

"Maybe a sweet little fruit bat," said Wes, grinning. "On a good day."

I was seeing another side of him as we prepared for surgery, I realised; of course, his adrenaline was building, giving him energy for the work ahead. It was refreshing to see, and charming, too.

Despite his new jovial demeanour, painful memories hovered in the periphery of my mind. I pushed them back, but they remained like a cluster of spectres as we chatted. A tubby girl with frizzy hair, trussed up in her boarding school band kid uniform – playing, of all things, the clarinet. I could easily relate to the whole bullying thing, but I didn't want Wes to think of me that way. If he laughed, it would sting – and I couldn't help compare that to the way my ex had laughed at me, not long before we broke up for good. I'd been due to start my internship on the neonatal unit and had been nervously munching my way through every comfort food imaginable; sure enough, the tubby band girl in me was resurfacing, adding on a few pounds that I had worked desperately hard to shift through diet and exercise.

Graham, my snooty pharmacist boyfriend, had asked if I'd stepped on any scales lately – or was I worried they might collapse beneath me? The laughter that followed had been the beginning of the end for us. Shame. My parents had liked

Graham; considered him to be a reliable Steady-Eddy. He'd seemed like a sure thing when it came to pleasing mum and dad – but me? Not so much. I missed his cruelty about as much as I missed his selfishness in the bedroom and inability to press any of my sexual buttons.

No, this tubby band kid was staying single, much to my mother and father's relief, I was sure.

"Lost in thought, Dr Hurst?"

I looked up at Wes, realising I'd gone into a kind of trance. I smiled weakly. "Just preparing myself, getting my head in the game." I cleared my throat. "Oh, and...call me Jen, would you?"

Wes smiled briefly. "You'll be fascinated, Jen. Trust me. Once you begin in plastics, there's no going back. I'm just relieved I could get you into theatre *on time*."

Wes cocked an eyebrow that made me blush – he really, really wasn't going to let my poor time-keeping go, was he? Just as I was beginning to like him, too. I sensed we'd turned a corner, and respect was building between us.

Wes turned on the spot and stopped abruptly, as if in surprise. I saw who was standing right behind him, holding aloft his surgical apron with a face like bitterness incarnate. Janine.

"Ah, prompt as ever," said Wes, holding his arms out while she dressed him, mindfully avoiding his freshly scrubbed hands. She helped him on with his gloves, too, her lips pressed in a firm line.

"Could we keep the banter to a minimum?" asked Janine in a stiff, unfriendly voice. "This is a serious environment and I like to ensure we keep it professional in the OR – first-time nerves not withstanding."

She glared at me as she made her way to the racks of pre-prepared surgical trays, which she would have gathered and signed off while we were meeting with Eric. I wondered if she only needed a little encouragement. As Wes entered the theatre to meet with his surgical colleagues, I wandered over to where Janine was preparing our tools in neat accessible rows. She side-eyed me, her eyebrows narrowing.

"Can I help you?"

"You've got a good system here," I said, nodding at the equipment. "Nice."

She looked up at me, shaking her head. "Are you *deliberately* trying to annoy me?"

I blinked. "No. I was just trying to lighten the mood – "

"Let me tell you something," said Janine, holding up a pair of gleaming tongs and wagging them like an admonishing finger at me. "My mood does not need lightening. My mood is none of your business. My job is to keep this OR functioning like clockwork, you get me? That means you do your job and let me get on with mine."

"All right, all right," I said, sighing.

Janine lifted the tray up onto the trolley. "Just stay out of my way, and we'll get along just fine."

She pushed her trolley of equipment into the theatre, leaving me standing there, quite perplexed.

♥

Working alongside Wes and I during this surgery was Dr Connie Bingham, an orthopaedics intern ahead of me who was specialising in bone grafts in particular. Connie would be crafting a piece of Eric's hip to fit his jaw. I watched, fascinated, as she sawed and filed away at the bone piece, creating a new piece of skull in the precise shape and size required. She had gleaming, deep mahogany skin and a serene face as she worked, like a carpenter deep in thought as she sculpted away.

She held the bone up to the light, turning it so I could see the smooth, rounded edges, forming the perfect fit.

"These are the bolts we'll be fixing to it – see how they move on hinges?" Dr Bingham held up an example in her free hand, letting the hinges flex before my eyes. Like a little piece of honeycomb, the diamond shapes would be screwed into place, allowing the bone to be attached with enough flexibility to allow for the precision required. Any bone graft fitted poorly would result in pain and suffering for Eric, so it was important to get the attachment right.

"That is truly a thing of beauty," I said, receiving the piece of bone and turning it in my hands.

"Now you can help me extract the vein from Eric's thigh – we're going to replace it with some tubing and use the one we take out to create a blood supply in his face," said Dr Bingham.

"Stealing my thunder, as per usual, Dr Bingham," said Wes, as he continued with his removal of the exposed tumour in Eric's cheek. "Perhaps I can lure you away from her craftsmanship long enough for you to actually get a look at this tumour, Jennifer?"

Wes' eyes glimmered magnificently under the headlight he wore, picking out the deep greens and flecks of yellow in each iris. My heart pounded as he drew me in closer to him, allowing me to tuck in, with his arms working around me. His voice was soft, with a slight lisp that gave me tingles, as he explained the excision of the tumour.

"The trick is to determine which parts of the mass are functioning tissue, and which are tumour. This one is fibrous and hard in some areas, and soft in others. See how it has attached itself to everything? The key is to prize it away, keeping it intact as you can, while avoiding these nerves here." Wes gestured with the tools between his fingers, using them like pointing sticks.

The sight of the tumour surrounded by green surgical paper was fascinating, but I couldn't help but recognise the warmth of Wes' hard body behind mine, almost pressing against my back. I found myself wishing he would curl himself around me, enveloping me in his warm embrace.

It was probably one of the more inappropriate thoughts I'd had during surgery.

"Now, you're already experienced surgically – I'm confident you can take over," he said.

"My pleasure," I said, continuing the work he had started. I removed the rest of the tumour precisely and dropped it piece by piece into the awaiting kidney-shaped dish.

"Very good," said Wes over my shoulder, once again making the hairs on my arms stand on end.

I assisted with the replacement of the vein, too, and its attachment in Eric's face. Using his own living components would be his best chance of creating a lasting blood flow, ensuring that his new bone graft would be accepted by the body and wouldn't turn necrotic. Once Eric was sewn up, we waited with baited breath as Wes used the blood-flow detector to determine whether the operation had been a success. If we couldn't detect any flow, then we'd have to open him back up again and investigate, causing more suffering for Eric.

Wes clucked his tongue, watching the monitor. "Fuck's sake," he muttered, as the numbers remained on zero. It was detecting nothing.

"Battery? Signal?" asked Dr Bingham.

"It's fully charged. Why aren't we detecting the bastard-poxy-blood-flow?"

Janine moved some of the tools away, making more room for Wes. He flinched as the tools clacked together.

"Quiet." He snapped, making Janine do a double-take. She caught my eye as she moved away, glaring as if it was somehow my fault that he'd lost his patience with her.

"Shit," he said, shaking his head in despair. "This can't be right. How can there be *zero* blood-flow? There's something up with the machine."

"Hang on a minute," I said, noticing an obvious problem. Eric's head was bent slightly forward – I could bet good money that his position was obstructing the flow and the machine's detection of it. I gently lifted Eric's head and watched the monitor bleep and flood into life and colour, lighting up with readings of a strong, clear, blood-flow.

"It's always the simple things," I said, re-positioning Eric and stepping away.

Dr Bingham chuckled. "Nicely done, Dr Hurst."

Wes was smiling broadly beneath his surgical mask. His scar appeared like a bolt of lightning in the nook between his cheek and the bridge of his nose, jagged and yet beautiful.

"Nicely done indeed, Jennifer," he said. Endorphins flooded my body. His praise could fast become addictive.

Momentarily his deep green eyes left the monitor and looked at me, studying me, as if finally, truly, seeing me.

My pulse quickened and I held my breath, my heart thumping beneath my scrubs.

One day. I'd spent one day shadowing Dr Brookes, and already I had seen him in multiple lights; loathing him one moment, and wanting to impress him the next.

Now my heart was fluttering at the sight of him, especially when he fixed his verdant eyes on me.

CHAPTER FOUR

Wesley

Jennifer had been my intern for almost a month now, acting first as my little shadow, before quickly becoming my fully-fledged assistant. One day, if she chose to stay in plastics, she would outshine me – I had no doubts about that whatsoever. A deep admiration was building within me, verging dangerously close to something more. Much, much more.

I had hoped that with the passing of time, my attraction to Jennifer would become easier to bear. I was now realising just how wrong I was on that front. With every shift spent together, I had only found more and more reason to appreciate her; all aspects of her.

Despite her rocky start, Jen had proved to be a deeply intelligent junior surgeon, who was attentive, curious, daring...everything I had ever dreamed my intern to be. She had a youthful optimism about modern medicine that was refreshing for me, confirming everything I already knew – that what we did was important, worthy of her awe. Even magical.

And now as the weekend approached, I had something very, very important to ask of her. I could only hope that she wouldn't laugh me into shameful oblivion when she discovered what it was.

"Your tea, and today's schedule," said Janine, passing my steaming mug and the rota sheet over the nurses' work station.

"Much obliged, as always," I said, taking my first blissfully hot gulp. As the liquid gold entered my body, I felt myself relax. Now I could think straight and plan my strategy for Jen. My breaths came quicker as I scanned the rota, wondering how I would even begin to approach the subject with her. I drummed my fingertips on the body of the mug I held.

"Are you okay, Wes?" asked Janine, pausing with her felt pen at the ready. She had already wiped the board clean, ready to write up our surgeries for the day and the times they were due to commence.

I pinched the bridge of my nose, feeling the reassuring ridge of my scar beneath my thumb that always grounded me.

"You know what – I think I'll take these to

my office. I've, er – I've a slight headache this morning. Would you send Jennifer straight to me when she gets here?"

"Of course," said Janine, rolling her eyes. "*When* she gets here."

I clucked my tongue. "She's infuriating with her timekeeping, I know. But she's already proving herself to be a very, very promising surgeon. You should give her a chance, Janine."

Janine scoffed, dissolving into a chuckle. "After the way she reacted to you that day? Please."

I rolled my eyes, taking another sip of delicious hot tea. It was what I called surgeon's tea; slopped together hastily, stewed a little too long or too short, with either too much or too little semi-skimmed milk. The perfect mug of tea was decidedly imperfect, and Janine had gotten it down to a surprising art. Janine knew my tea should never, ever be quite *right* – or else it wasn't surgeon's tea.

Just as she kept the routines I depended on – delivering my tea and schedule exactly the way I wanted her to – Janine could be relied on in many other ways, both clinically and personally. One way was her undying loyalty to me – one that made her particularly, let's say, protective of me. It was endearing, and I was grateful to her for her support – no matter that I, of course, needed no such protection. The fact remained that she hadn't gelled at all with Jennifer, and I was keen to change that.

"She explained that to me. I'll have you know that she thinks I'm *handsome*," I said, taking a satisfied swig.

Janine spun back around to face me, popping the lid back on her pen. She drummed her trimmed red nails on the station worktop.

"Really. Did she say that?"

"She did," I said, unable to hide the smugness lifting the corners of my mouth into a slight smile.

Janine raised her eyebrows, looking down at her hands. "Well, that's inappropriate for an intern."

"Nonsense," I said brusquely. "It was music to my ears. Send her down to me the minute she gets here, won't you?"

I retreated to my office, my thoughts once again returning to Jen and how I would begin to say what I needed to say. It was a delicate proposition to say the least. She would either laugh at me, respond with absolute disgust and file a formal complaint...or she'd assist me with my problem. I'd make it worth her while, certainly. She had more than proved herself worthy of the gift I was going to give her in exchange: unlimited access to my surgeries, barring none, with an opportunity for hands-on involvement in each of them. Eventually, she would be leading them, and she could graduate from the surgical programme with a full endorsement from me.

I couldn't say fairer than that. Most interns were lucky just to observe for the first year. Jen had more than sufficient experience in Hartcliffe's neonatal surgery pathway to justify my propulsion of her along my programme, which settled any ethical quandaries from my end. I could only hope she'd accept the challenge I was going to put before her, rather than laugh in my miserable face.

The door was gingerly opened behind me with a creak of the old hinges. I rose up and turned quickly to see the crown of Jen's golden hair as she bowed inside, closing the door behind her.

"Dr Hurst," I said, licking my dry lips. Despite my lifetime of becoming comfortable with my facial difference, I still found myself searching Jen's face for her reaction. Did she consider my scar a disfigurement that marred me? Did it repel her, in spite of what she said – that I was, in her eyes, handsome?

The word had played on my mind ever since she'd said it. I was ashamed of that; as if my ego needed any more building up. Why, then, did I cling so desperately to that judgement of me? I realised, in that moment as Jen's eyes met mine, that it wasn't so much the word – it was the fact it came from her. The fact that *she'd* said it.

It wasn't as if she were the only woman to ever find me attractive. My scar hadn't deterred Rebecca, for instance – though she had asked me to consider corrective surgery to neaten it up, a comment that had wounded me more than she'd have ever known. As a matter of pride, I'd shrugged it off as a harmless misunderstanding, and yet – little had I known – it did reflect her feelings about me. That I fell below her expectations.

"Janine said you wanted to see me right away," said Jen, smiling up at me with her dazzling eyes. "I'm sorry I'm late. My bathroom flooded back at the flat and the tube was rammed – "

I sighed, folding my arms across my chest.

"More excuses?"

Jen had the grace to look up at me sheepishly, knowing that her time-keeping was god-awful and my one and only bug-bear with her practice. As a surgeon, she was coming along in leaps and bounds, tackling each new task with vigour and enthusiasm...but her arrival to the ward was on a constant delay each morning. It wasn't good enough.

"I'm sorry, Wes. I don't know what's wrong with me," she said. "I'm not late every day. And if I am, it's only a few minutes – "

Now she was annoying me, to the point where I almost forgot that I was going to ask an enormous favour from her.

"Dr Hurst, good time-keeping – "

" – is a cornerstone of good practice as a surgeon and as a medical professional in general," Jen said, finishing my motto for me. It frustrated me so that I almost wanted to flick the woman away like a bug.

"*Why* do you infuriate me like this?" I raised my voice, making her eyebrows rise up under her wispy fringe of hair. "You – you've cut your hair." I was abruptly sidetracked as I noticed the difference in her.

Now she cocked an eyebrow, running her fingers through her ponytail.

"I had some layers put in, some face-framing, and a long fringe. I'm amazed you noticed it," said Jen, flushing pink in the cheeks. "I'm glad I could shock you out of scolding me, for once."

I blinked my thoughts away, stopping myself short of telling her that *of course* I'd noticed, that I noticed everything, always, especially if it pertained to her. That I wanted to see her with her hair down, wearing absolutely nothing else. Maybe one of my surgical scrub shirts.

"Listen – look, there's – "

"Dr Brookes?"

I paced the room, realising I didn't have any

grasp on this at all. Jen could – and likely would – laugh at me, and I would have to withstand her judgement and explain myself like a man.

"I've got something I need to ask of you, and I – I'm afraid I can't hazard a guess at how you might respond," I said, inwardly wincing. I sounded like a coward, and I knew it.

To my surprise, Jen looked intrigued. I was so taken aback that I let a silence grow between us as I studied the interest in her gaze. Jen stepped forward, placing a hand on my forearm. The touch of her delicate, manicured fingertips made me flinch as if her touch burned me.

Her eyes met mine, steady, assured.

"So, just ask me," she said softly.

She was in my space now; the scent and warmth radiating from her was mesmerising. I focused on her plump pink lips, suddenly wishing I could summon up the courage to kiss them. I'd need more than courage to fight the law suit she could bring against me if I sprang myself on her like that. Instead I cleared my throat, running my fingers through my tangled hair.

"Wes, just ask me," she repeated, licking her lips very gently. I became fixated on the gentle moisture glistening on the surface, begging me to dive greedily in.

"Do you – do you know what I'm going to ask?"

She couldn't possibly know. That was madness. Yet her expression told me she was sure of it, whatever it was, and now I was intrigued as well.

"I think I do," she said, taking another step forward until she was as close as possible.

She looked up at me now, unsure and uneasy. Yet her fingers left my arm and reached up to my face, her fingertip tracing the scar from beneath my nose, down to the top of my lip. I shivered at her touch, feeling it in my groin as her hand curled around my jaw and drew me down to meet her. I found myself holding in a breath as it caught in my throat.

A sudden rush of adrenaline overcame me as Jen's head tipped backward, her lips all at once meeting mine. Warm, firm, and full.

She kissed so softly, so tantalisingly, that I couldn't hold myself back for long. I pulled her to me by the shoulders and wrapped her in my arms, my hands finding fistfuls of her golden, silky hair. Jen groaned against my lips as I devoured her, cradling her in my arms. Her lips gave way to my tongue as I explored her sweet, soft mouth, drawing it out, tasting her like the delicious thing she was.

As our lips softly parted, we remained nose to nose, our chests heaving.

"Is that what you were going to ask me?" she

said, panting softly, her lips curling into a smile.

Whatever wonderful thing had just happened couldn't have been further from my mind when I'd asked her to meet me here – that she could want to kiss me, her mentor? A gentle laugher rumbled from within me as the fog of lust began to finally clear.

"No, not at all."

She blinked, her brow knitting in confusion even as her smile faded. Some sort of spell was at risk of breaking.

"What were you going to ask me, then?" She stepped away, withdrawing from me.

I swallowed hard, the awkwardness returning despite the fact that the woman of my dreams was literally – quite inexplicably – in my arms. I struggled a moment to find the words, still distracted by the sudden, but very welcome, intimacy between us.

"It's complicated, and a little risky. My parents are in town, and I...I wanted you to stand in as my partner. My romantic partner, that is."

"You – what? Stand in? You're not making any sense."

"It'd make sense if you knew my sentimental old mother and father.' I took in a deep breath and blew it out slowly, folding my arms. "In exchange for a well-deserved fast-track along the programme, I want you to pose as my girlfriend,"

I said. "I know it's a little left-field, and unconventional, but I need this favour to put their minds at ease and I think it's a fair swap." My voice was hoarse, my throat tight, but I kept to the facts.

Jen's face twisted in confusion, and then very apparent anger. *Oh, bollocks,* I thought. *You've done it now, Brookes. Here comes the law suit.*

"You...you want me to do *what*?"

Jen's hands rose to my chest and began to push me forcefully away when the office door creaked loudly open. Our heads turned abruptly to see Janine, holding a glass of water and two paracetamol in her open palm.

" – got these here, for that headache of yours, Wes." Janine's words fell away from her as she saw us there, half-embracing, our faces flushed. Janine dropped the glass and it bounced on the linoleum, the water pooling at our feet.

CHAPTER FIVE

Jennifer

Fresh air blessed me as I made my way outside, desperate to get my head around what had happened that morning. Persevering through several multi-disciplinary surgeries after that awkward encounter had not been easy, but it was a definite lesson in keeping my head on straight and prioritising our patients' safety.

I called Clara's number the moment I left the grounds, praying she was available. Her schedule as a social worker was pretty rammed, but ever since we'd become friends, she'd assured me she would be there for me in a crisis. I was pretty sure this warranted the crisis label.

When she answered by video call, I looked up at the sky and mouthed the words *thank you*.

"Hey, Jen – you okay?"

I swept my fringe away and placed my hand

on my forehead, sighing. "No, I'm not okay. I think I've just made a complete twat of myself to my boss and – oh god, I thought he *wanted me* and at least, I don't know, *respected me*, and my progress, but apparently – "

"Woah, woah, slow down. You look – " her face came closer to the camera, observing me with a frown. I could see the busy street behind her – she was leaving work. "Are you crying?"

"I might be," I said, furiously wiping away a stray tear.

"All right – do we need some hard liquor or a cosy coffee for this one?"

I thought about it, letting the April breeze cool my face down a little. Despite recent events, I had no intentions of doing a midnight flit, packing up my room and disappearing to another country. I was dedicated to my career, and committed to the surgical programme in plastics. That meant I was committed to Dr Brookes, the dreamy-kissing arsehole that he was. It also meant that I would be back here bright and early tomorrow – hopefully with a damn game plan – and I did *not* need a hangover to contend with on top of everything else.

"Definitely coffee," I said, pulling my jacket around my waist. "If you're near Islington, we can meet at my place, though I doubt I'll have any privacy from my flat-mates."

"No, no," said Clara, waving her car keys at the camera. "I was in the office today. I can meet you at Gina's for the good stuff."

"I'm so glad you said that," I said, letting out a sigh of relief. "Because I can't face the shop right now and I definitely ran out of milk this morning. Are you...did you *drive* to the office? No chauffeured car offered by hubby today, then?"

Clara's husband was a barrister with a personal family fortune in the billions. I was quite certain she didn't need to be driving her *old reliable* car anymore.

Clara scoffed, blowing a raspberry with her full lips. "I'll never give up old Bessie. She's a part of me. Meet you there in thirty minutes?"

"I'll get the drinks in," I said.

I took a long swig of my frothy mocha after explaining the whole sorry scene, wishing I could curl up under the faux-fur rug we were seated on and hide from my own shame. The crackling fireplace and heady scent of the coffee machine weren't helping, lulling me almost to sleep. Still, I was safe and warm in the company of a good friend now; she'd help me out of this. She had to.

"So you just assumed he wanted to kiss you?" asked Clara. "That's impressive. You go, Jen."

"He *did* kiss me! Full-on romantic-movie-dipping-me-on-a-mountain-top kissing! I felt it –

" I looked around me at the other patrons and hushed my voice. " – I felt it everywhere. But that isn't what I thought he was going to ask me. I *thought* he wanted to ask me on a date."

"I'm confused. I thought your plastic surgeon was known for being an arsehole?"

"He is," I said, curling my legs up inside my leather armchair. "He's also fascinating, dominant, stubborn, wonderful. He's got these endearing ways about him, and we've got these unspoken tensions between us that've been growing like freaking knotweed over the last month. And with his patients, he's a real softy. He's a tyrant with his staff – he's especially hard on me when he needs to be."

"Sounds like he was earlier," said Clara with a smirk.

I drew out my leg and nudged her with my foot, making her laugh.

"Ssh. I thought he was always being *hard* on me because it was his way of connecting with me, maybe. Now I feel like a prized idiot, knowing that he only saw me as a good potential prop to reassure his parents. He's infuriating. He has these finicky little ways – these routines he's obsessed with. Always the same every morning. A mug of tea and a copy of his schedule, which he already knows because he has a digital version – "

"Wait, *you* don't make the tea, do you?"

I rolled my eyes. "No. His charge nurse does it, though god knows why. She doesn't need to be his skivvy, but she seems to enjoy it. They've got this, I don't know...this bond, I guess. They've worked together for years. Anyway, he hates things being even a little out of place, and that's why I thought he was struggling to ask me. So I thought I'd...help."

"And not only are you angry about him seeing you like a prop, but you think you've made a fool of yourself?"

"I know I have."

"No you haven't, honey. Is Brookes neurodivergent, by any chance?"

"Oh god yes," I said, swallowing another mouthful of delicious mocha. I was feeling soothed and better already. "But we're doctors. He's a surgeon, for Christ's sake. Show me one who isn't a little divergent in one sense or another."

"Point taken," said Clara, setting her mug down on the coffee table. "This charge nurse of his – you think they might be – ?"

I shrugged, feeling completely lost. "They could be, but I doubt it somehow. She seems utterly dedicated to him. She certainly seemed appalled when she found us."

"She's got the hots for him, guarantee it," said Clara. "If she's smashing glasses, she's obsessed. She'd probably jump at the chance to be his pretend-girlfriend and please the 'rents."

I smirked, shaking my head fondly. Clara always had a way of lightening the mood. "She did not smash the glass, she dropped it in surprise."

"This is all besides the point, anyway. The question is – are you going to do it?"

I blinked. "What? You can't be serious."

"I'm deadly serious. He's humiliated you – are you going to let him get away with that? If you take on this role, you'll get in on all the surgical action, *and* you can mess with him a little," said Clara.

"I'm not sure I'm happy about screwing with him *or* messing with his parents. I just wanted to complete the programme and get on with my career," I said, wiping my face in despair. I rested my hand on my jaw, leaning on the arm of my chair for support.

"You want to let him ask the charge nurse and give her all the fun?"

She had a point, there. Something told me Janine would relish the opportunity to play house with Dr Brookes, and she'd treated me with nothing but disdain since I'd arrived in plastics. If I did pretend to be his partner, I could piss both her and Wes off at my leisure, get my own back, and hold him to the fire if he didn't keep his promise about the surgeries.

Suddenly it didn't sound like a bad deal at

all.

"Not to mention the fact that you'll actually get to meet the parents. Surely you're curious about who raised this scary-sexy guy with the finicky ways you keep telling me about?" Clara asked.

All right, she had me there. I was *very* curious about what kind of people Wes Brookes' parents would be. How do you raise a man like him, anyway?

"Come on, let's get an Irish coffee and push the boat out a little. I feel like celebrating," I said with a satisfied grin.

♥

It was early morning. I sucked in a deep breath as I entered the plastics ward, knowing I would see Wes at the nurses' station, mug of tea and schedule in-hand. We were due to have our first post-op meeting with Eric this morning, and I was looking forward to seeing him and reviewing his healing process. Nothing was going to drag me down today; I'd decided that already, even if I did feel foolish and a little bruised from our encounter yesterday. The kiss, though – that full embrace, his biceps surrounding my shoulders, his mouth on mine...that had been real, hadn't it? There had been no misunderstanding when my lips touched his and he'd responded with enough gusto to knock me off my feet.

What happened after was still the elephant in the room, regardless of the kiss. Before our shift began, I needed to deal with the bizarre, left-of-field offer that Wes had made me; the one I'd run from initially, before feeling inspired to give him a taste of his own medicine. I could only hope there was still time to say yes.

He was there; of course he was. Broad-shoulders in green scrubs, receiving his tea and a copy of the rota. My heart leapt to see him there, so still and composed, knowing I had made him breathless with my kiss just yesterday, and he'd made me feel...all kinds of things. I only wished I knew what had come over me to make me so bold. Maybe it was the proximity; maybe I was a glutton for his punishment. That would explain why I was so late all the time, despite priding myself on my professional conduct at all times. Clearly, I *wanted* him to tell me off.

Maybe it was that sexy jagged scar that broke up his handsome, chiselled face like a statue that had been split apart and repaired, giving him a look of wisdom, sophistication. The scar that drew my eye line straight down to his lips that I wanted to suck and pull on with my teeth.

But it didn't matter now. Now he'd think I was a loose woman who'd just wanted a quick fling and was downright brazen about it. My only chance at getting my own back was to do exactly as Clara suggested; to harness the opportunity that was presented before me and mess with him a little – once I'd grasped the details.

"Dr Brookes," I said, making his shoulders visibly stiffen as the words left my mouth and met his ears. "Could I have a moment in your office, please? I arrived early to make sure we had enough time."

Janine scowled at me, her eyes glaring beneath the arching of her perfectly filled-in eyebrows.

"Good morning, Janine." I smiled, passing the nurses' station to make my way to Wes' office. I would have to keep my cool and be the absolute professional if I didn't want to give my true intentions away.

"I'll be just a moment, Jen," he said softly, taking a sip of his tea as his eyes scanned the day's rota.

As I slipped into Wes' office and quietly closed the door, I took the opportunity to really look around the small, sparsely furnished room. His desk and shelves were of course immaculate, with only a juicy green succulent in a small grey pot and a framed photograph occupying the shelves. Oh, almost – there were some old lever arch files neatly lined up on the far left, looking as though they hadn't been opened in years, and yet devoid of any dust.

Typical Wes. Not a speck of dirt or dust to be

found, and nothing out of place.

I stopped at the desk and glanced up at the framed photograph. It was of an older couple, taken maybe 30 years ago, judging by the age of the picture. The tall, Nordic-looking man was the spitting image of Wes, blonde hair and all. They were on the grounds of an estate; maybe a National Trust place or somewhere like that, with verdant topiary in the background the same colour as Wes' eyes. The three of them were smiling fondly with a boy of about 13 crouching down between them. The boy had wavy dark blonde hair and skinny legs in red shorts. A distinctive scar meandered from his top lip, under his nose, and up toward his eye. The boy was grinning with wonky teeth, and between his legs was a small shaggy grey dog, tongue lolling.

There was a little collar with a tag and a name on it. I wondered if I could reach up and take the photo down to get a better look at it.

"Dusty," came Wes' voice behind me, making me flinch. "I never did get over losing that boy. He was my best friend in the whole world."

I turned, shaking slightly at almost being caught. Well, I guess I was caught – but weren't photos meant for looking at?

"He's a cute dog," I said, seeing Wes smile in fondness at the memory. It warmed my heart unexpectedly to see such a genuine smile on his usually serious, almost permanently scowling face. Only privately, when alone with me, had he been allowing for more smiles, and even laughter, to feature in his communications.

"There never was a finer pup. I was supposed to be a vet – that's what I thought I was going to be, at that age. My parents used to joke that I was a sentimental old soul. They're both surgeons, of course. When Dusty died, the idea of becoming a vet went completely out the window. I couldn't face seeing another animal put to sleep," said Wes, his voice fading to almost a whisper.

"I'm so sorry, Wes," I said, realising this conversation was already not going how I'd planned it. Why was my heart thumping like that? Why did I want to throw my arms around Wes and comfort him, as if he was still the little boy in the photograph?

"No matter," said Wes, twirling his empty mug by the handle.

"If it's any consolation, both of my parents are surgeons, too. I didn't have a whole lot of choice about what to become if I wanted their respect," I said, my stomach turning in knots just at the thought of David and Alison, and the ways they'd admonished me if I didn't achieve well enough in my exams.

"Boarding school?" asked Wes.

"You bet," I said. "Clarinet in the band, too.

Ugly uniform."

Wes snorted with laughter. "I played the piano myself. Missed my parents dreadfully when I was boarding. I couldn't wait for the holidays."

"Wish I could say the same," I said. "School was better than being picked on at home by my mum and dad." I rolled my eyes, remembering it all-too-well.

"That's a shame," said Wes, placing his mug down on the desk – on a coaster, no less – and standing before me. His scent of clean linen and shampoo washed over me, making my body sigh.

"Listen, speaking of parents...you never did answer my proposition. I respect that we were, erm – well, perhaps there was some confusion on both our parts –"

"A moment of madness," I said, looking up at his dazzling green eyes and long lashes. "Think nothing of it."

"Quite, quite," said Wes, a deep frown taking over his face. He looked down at the floor, wringing his hands. "My parents are in town this weekend. They're the loveliest, most supportive parents I could ever have wished for, but, uh – they have a morbid fear that I'm going to die alone. Past relationships ended rather badly, and since then – well, my work – "

"Understood," I said, knowing all too well what a lifesaver work was when everything was falling apart in your personal life. I'd gone through the same with Graham. His previous relationships, though – now those intrigued me. A part of me wanted to ask him to elaborate; another part of me knew how intrusive that would be.

"Yes, exactly – you understand." Wes sighed, rubbing his large hand on the back of his neck. "Well, I was rather hoping you might jump at the opportunity to speed through the programme a little faster, and that you might feel better about doing me such an intrusive favour if there was something in it for you. You're an experienced intern with years under your belt already; I've no doubt about your abilities whatsoever. From what I've seen of you this last month, I think you've every shot at being an excellent plastic surgeon."

A lump sat in my throat, making me swallow hard. I had to look down and blink away tears. "Thank you, Wes."

"But in exchange for a little boost along the pathway – I need someone to help me convince my parents that I'm not wasting away here, and that my personal life isn't in ruins." He cleared his throat gruffly, folding his arms. "I see them so rarely that I'm sure I could concoct some story about us parting ways down the line. But for now, it'd really make them happy to see me with a beautiful fellow surgeon by my side."

Now was the time for me to hide my smirk as I accepted the offer, but I found myself feeling entirely different. A warmth was tumbling away in my belly; a nervous excitement making my mouth curl into a smile. He thought I was an excellent surgeon. He thought I was beautiful.

"Of course, I accept," I said, holding out my hand for him to shake. The look of astonishment on his face was endearing. "I think I can handle those two in the photograph."

Wes took my hand and shook it, his eyes studying mine with a gratitude that made them sparkle. He held my hand a while longer, his thumb stroking my palm as he gradually let go. He gave me shivers, reigniting the same feelings that had knocked me off me feet when we'd kissed.

"That's settled, then."

"Looks like it is."

"I'll let them know to set another place for you at the dinner table," said Wes. "I'll have Janine give you the details of the family home in Knightsbridge."

Suddenly he was back to sounding clinical, matter-of-fact. I distinctly felt the little sparks of magic fizzling away. Worse than that, I was perplexed – why the hell did he need Janine to behave like his personal PA, forwarding me address details?

I asked him as much, with an incredulous look on my face. I didn't see what she had to do with anything.

"Because that's what I do," he said. "I delegate to her and she sees that it gets done. She won't know about our plans – that's strictly between us. Shall we, then? Eric and his mother will be waiting for our assessment."

I didn't get it. I didn't get it at all. There was a strange loyalty between them that was frankly inappropriate in my opinion. As we made our way into the hall together, I bit my tongue, struggling not to say words to that effect. If he was so hell-bent on involving her, even in some small way, why didn't he ask her to be his fake-girlfriend instead of me?

♥

The meeting with Eric was a huge success. His face had healed beautifully, the graft settling in as if it had always been there. He was seeing the physio team to help him build his facial muscles and learn to smile and speak clearly again, and he was making sound progress. To think that I had held that piece of bone in my hand, which now formed a major part of his skull, was astonishing to me. I could see why Wes so loved what he did . It was pure brilliance. We were changing lives.

As I left to grab a drink from the canteen, Janine stepped into my path. Her expression was a joy to behold as always. She gave me a card with the Kensington address printed on it with a day and a time: Saturday, 7.00 p.m.

There was even a dress code: smart/casual.

"The Kensington house – that's one of Wes', right?" she asked, her eyes narrowing almost to slits. She tipped her head to one side as if trying to work me out. "It's the one he grew up in before his parents moved to the Surrey house."

I wasn't going to give her the satisfaction of knowing she was bothering me at all, but it did irk me that she knew such intimate details about Wes. This was still our business, not hers.

"That's for me to know," I said coolly. "But thanks for this."

"No problem," she said through gritted teeth, looking suitably irritated by my brush-off.

Maybe she was used to knowing everything about Wes' business, but if he hadn't seen fit to tell her about our plans to present me as his girlfriend to his parents, then I certainly wasn't going to tell her.

As I left at the end of the day's shift, I focused on the plan I'd concocted with Clara, reminding myself that I was *not* just dutifully following Wes' request like a dummy. I had a little trick planned which would surely put a bat up their nightdress and at least create some entertainment for me. Crucially, it would remind Wes not to mess with my feelings.

Why, then, did I still feel so damn nervous about it? Why did my hands shake as I put the key in the lock of my front door, picturing the first impression I might make to Mr and Mrs Brookes? It wasn't as if I was really, *really* meeting his parents.

It wasn't as if I was getting my heart involved.

CHAPTER SIX

Wesley

An emergency call-out on a Saturday morning - *the* Saturday. Well, I reasoned it was preferable to finding myself lost in thought at the gym, agonising over my kiss with Jennifer. Here, it was impossible to focus too long on anything except saving the patient – and this patient was in dire need of our help, or he'd die on the table. I had to act swiftly, call in the correct support, and focus on the emergency reconstruction.

And to think that my most pressing concern had been the evening's dinner with my parents.

I scrubbed my hands and arms thoroughly, getting my head in the game as Janine prepared my surgical gown and readied our tools. Jen was already scrubbed in and assisting Dr Connie Bingham with stabilising the patient and assessing his injuries.

"How is our patient doing, nurse?" I asked Janine, calling out over the gushing of the taps.

"He's critical, but they've got him under control, just about. Brief run-down from Bingham and Hurst is that he has extensive burns to the left side of the face, facial fractures from the fall and potential damage to the brain – he landed on a concrete surface," said Janine, helping me on with my gloves.

"They've sent Mr Griffin in from Barts to deal with the head trauma."

"Griffin? Jesus, it's been a while," I said, unable to remember when I'd last worked with him. Another emergency, another time.

Janine gave me a brief run-down of our patient as she hurriedly helped me gown-up. 16 year old Aleksander Brosko had been out all night, drinking and goofing off with friends. Someone had the bright idea of daring Alex to climb the pylon above an overground rail-track, resulting in facial fractures, head trauma, and extensive burns from the electrical blast. It would be a multidisciplinary effort to save him, requiring all hands on deck.

"Tell me Griffin's in there already."

"He's performing the craniotomy as we speak," said Janine. "Subdural haematoma."

A moment later and I was gowned up at Mr Griffin's side, assessing the damage to the boy's face; he'd suffered extensive fracturing from a crushing impact, consistent with a fall from a height against a concrete surface – at an angle, too. His burns were extensive, and would require grafts at a later date.

For now, it was a case of doing what we could to deal with the worst and stabilise him in the time we had.

Dr Hurst and Dr Bingham had commenced fluid resuscitation and were cleaning the wounds for access.

"Jen, you'll be dealing with the bone fragments," I said, stepping aside. "Come and stand here."

Alex was stabilised enough to be taken to the HDU, but he wasn't out of the woods yet. His treatment would be delivered in multiple stages, with multiple surgeries, no doubt, and he'd likely be spending weeks in Sacred Heart.

Janine returned from informing the family, who had gathered in the atrium, waiting for news. I would be with them momentarily to give them a proper run-down of the surgery and its outcomes.

"Dr Hurst was particularly on the ball throughout that surgery," said Janine in a blunt tone of voice, as she dumped her gown in the laundry bin. "Something's given *her* a spring in her step."

I couldn't help but smile, which only seemed to make Janine's scowl deepen all the more.

"You might as well know she's going to be taking on more of a hands-on role from now on," I said. "She's proven more than capable, so I'm speeding up her progress on the programme."

"Because she's capable, you say? Is that the only reason she's being given special treatment?" asked Janine, glaring obnoxiously as if to remind me of the awkward embrace she'd found us in.

I groaned inwardly, ripping off my gloves and disposing of them in the clinical waste bin. I sensed there was more to this than simple disappointment about my conduct in the workplace. This was personal. I tipped my head back and rolled it side to side on my shoulders until my neck cracked, considering her words carefully. It was obvious there was a very real jealousy emerging, and I couldn't have that. It was important that what Janine witnessed unfolding between myself and Jen didn't disrupt our overall cohesion as a team.

"Listen," I said, placing a reassuring hand on her shoulder.

"Please, Wes. I need to oversee Alex's transfer to the HDU." She attempted to shrug me off, but I stepped in front of her, blocking her path. Janine blushed, curiously, and seemed to struggle to meet my gaze.

"Listen to me," I said, taking her by the shoulders. "If my conduct lately has disappointed you, then...sod it. I apologise, all right?"

She looked at me, then, and seemed to relax under my hands, though she remained silent and uncharacteristically bashful.

"I couldn't make this department work without you."

Giving her a friendly pat on both shoulders, I left, hoping I'd smoothed things over. I took her silence as an acceptance, at least.

But as I left to see to the family, Janine's words rang in my ears all the same: *is that the only reason she's being given special treatment*? I couldn't help but question again if my propulsion of Jen along the programme was unethical after all. But she was my intern, damn it, and if I thought she was ready, she was ready.

As I took the empty lift down and found the opportunity to take a breather, I sighed deeply, leaning back against the hand rail. My mind wondered back to her. Jen had looked angelic with her blue eyes sparkling above her surgical mask, focusing on her tasks. Pulling my gaze from her was becoming a real struggle; apparently I was even finding opportune moments to admire her during critical surgery, for heaven's sake.

She was a fast learner, deftly executing her

duties as if she'd been doing them for years. And she had, in one sense, having worked already in the neonatal unit. I had to wonder why, exactly, Jen hadn't completed her surgical programme in the neonatal unit, despite there being no concerns about her practise. Why the last-minute jump to plastics, bringing her to me?

She could graduate on time with credits earned, but in terms of the discipline itself and the knowledge she'd already garnered, she'd have been much better off staying where she was. The two practises – neonatal and children's plastic surgery – were worlds apart.

It was as if she was delaying her career progression deliberately. I pondered more as the lift descended, folding my arms across my chest. Could it be there was something about the light at the end of that tunnel – of finally graduating to a fully-fledged surgical position – that scared her?

♥

Jen's mesmerising image came before me as she stepped beneath the lamplight on my parents' quiet, sleepy street. Her voluptuous curves were highlighted by the skin-tight black dress she wore, cutting a tantalising figure against the cold, white backdrop of the four-storey town houses.

The sound of her high heels clacking against the paving slabs gave me shivers with every confidant stride she took. I noticed the earrings sparkling by her long, swan-like neck, drawing my attention there. Her halter-neck dress gave her a bust that called to me too. My breathing became laboured as my pulse climbed, noticing the muscles in her calves and the way her high blonde ponytail bobbed just above her defined shoulder-blades.

That yearning returned; the impulse to grab, to kiss, to drag my lips along every part of her, starting with her neck. She looked stunning. Perfect. Leagues beyond wife material.

She was goddess material.

"You're here," she said breathily, stopping before the wrought iron gates of my parents' house. "I thought you'd be inside. God, you look – " she paused, as if struggling to catch her breath.

Her crystalline blue eyes scanned my hair, which I'd bothered to comb into waves, down to my black V-neck sweater and black tapered jeans. I'd brought a casual grey knitted jacket, which I had slung over one arm, and a bottle of plonk for the table.

"You look so h-handsome," she said eventually.

"So do you," I said, wincing inwardly. "I mean, er – that is, you look pretty breathtaking yourself. Not handsome, of course – "

Jen broke into a fit of laughter, looping her arm in mine. I felt some of the tension shifting; I was at least grateful for that. Even if I had made a prat of myself within seconds of us meeting.

"I find myself feeling…uncharacteristically nervous," I said as we made our way up the stairway, attractively paved in a chequerboard tile. We stopped before the stained glass doorway, arm in arm. One of her sparkly earrings caught my eye in my periphery, forcing me to glance down at her. She smiled, briefly, up at me.

"We can do this," she said, giving my arm a squeeze. "Piece of cake."

I couldn't tell her that it wasn't introducing her to my parents that made me nervous – especially knowing that we were presenting a completely phony image to the people I respected most. More, even, than my superiors in surgery. They'd taught me everything I knew, after all.

No, it was *her* that made me nervous. She was too beautiful…and too close. She made me want to pin her in the arch of the doorway and ravish that delicious neck of hers like a bloodthirsty vampire. My kisses would turn to a licking, a sucking, making my way down her chest to that ample bust –

I cursed myself for thinking about her so inappropriately. Jen deserved better than to be objectified like that. She was doing me a favour, for Christ's sake, and I was looking at her like a hungry wolf.

"Hey," said Jen, nudging me in the side. "You're pulling that constipated face you do when a vein doesn't take or a graft doesn't quite fit."

Laughter escaped me, and I relaxed again. Of its own volition, my hand wandered to the small of Jen's back, touching warm skin. This was the image I wanted to present to my parents when they opened the door; a casual intimacy between us. Only I hadn't realised how low the V of the back of her dress went, and I was very pleasantly surprised to feel skin. Did I feel a gentle mist of sweat beneath my fingertips? Was she enjoying my hand being there?

"I find myself feeling like a sort of...like a Jekyll and Hyde character around you, Jennifer," I said. My voice was thickened by the desire that I used every fibre of my being to force to the back of my mind. A hopeless task.

"What do you mean?" she asked, her voice almost a whisper as she gazed up at me. Even in her heels, the crown of her head barely reached my shoulder.

When I didn't answer, a slight frown appeared on her otherwise smooth forehead. She was so young, still. So unblemished. She'd never known a hair out of place, let alone –

"You mean like you want to promote me one minute, ravage me like a savage beast the next?" she chuckled. Her laughter faded away when I didn't answer, and she looked uncertain – almost afraid.

"Something like that," I said, feeling my resolve rapidly melting away, and desire taking its place.

My hand seemed to move on its own to cup her jaw. Despite the ferocious longing inside me, I found my touch was gentle. Jen's eyes became half-lidded as I found her lips and parted them, gliding my tongue against hers. Jen went limp in my embrace and groaned as I kissed her long and deep, letting go, just momentarily, to my own aching needs. Above our heads, the Tiffany lamp inside the archway of my parents' porch flooded us with soft, warm light.

How perfect, then, that the front door should open in that moment.

"Wesley!" came my father's voice with his Swedish accent. "Weren't you even going to ring the bell?"

Jen sprang from my arms, smoothing the frayed hairs from her forehead. I cleared my throat, taking the bottle of wine from my deep coat pocket. Well, at least that was the stiffness in my trousers taken care of – there would be no risk of my parents seeing anything they shouldn't.

"For you, dad, for the table," I said, my heart pounding.

Dad took the wine and glanced between it

and Jennifer, his round spectacles shining under the lamplight. Mum appeared beside him, snaking an affectionate arm around his waist.

"Never mind the wine, Wesley – who's this astonishing woman you've brought to our doorstep?" asked mum. "We knew you were bringing a – special guest, but –"

"Jen, these are my parents, Henrik and Oonagh. Mum, Dad, this is Dr Jennifer Hurst," I said, "My - "

"Fiancé," said Jennifer, holding her left hand out in front of her. A diamond I had never seen before sparkled under the porch light. I sucked in a sharp, quiet breath.

Damn it, what the hell was she *playing at*? I froze as the shock rippled through me. My parents would have a heart attack.

I bit my lip, my stomach churning in knots. My eyes were boring into Jennifer as she grinned with a false smugness, turning her hand this way and that with her manicured fingers spread out. Both my parents paused, watching the prisms catching in the light – and erupted into a gushing, whooping, celebratory dance in the doorway.

Oh, god help us all.

"You've DONE IT, my boy!"

"Congratulations, darling!"

My father embraced me first – head and

shoulders above me at 6"7 tall – before grabbing Jen by her bare shoulders and kissing both her cheeks. Mum hugged Jennifer and squeezed her like an old friend, before pulling me down to her height – closer to Jen's – and smacking a kiss on my forehead.

Jen appeared stunned, dizzied by the sudden commotion.

I suspected she'd thought she was pulling a cool trick with that ring, but she had no idea of the Pandora's box she'd just opened. She glanced at me uneasily, her eyes wide as she was pulled in for uncomfortable hugs. Despite my fury, I returned a brief, knowing smile which said *not such a smart-arse now, are we?*

My parents often caught people off guard, given my own reserved demeanour. I'd heard some people even described me as cold. Rebecca had certainly been taken aback by their obvious passion and energy, not realising that my personal disposition was a response to them. Not a deflection, but rather a long-ago-learned mode of self-preservation. Jennifer would have to learn just as Rebecca had – although of course, Jen wasn't really my girlfriend. Certainly not my fiancé.

As mum wiped stray tears from her eyes and dad guided us over the threshold with a sweep of his arm, I had to wonder what Jen's parents were like. She'd mentioned they picked on her, and I gathered there was little love between them. What stunt had she thought she was pulling with that false engagement ring? Had she expected my mum and dad to respond angrily?

Was she trying to give me a hard time, and incite anger from me?

Only her own parents could have given her that idea, because if she'd met mine for even a moment before now, she would have known that a surprise engagement would have quite the opposite effect. I was surprised we hadn't seen them hit the deck and needed to perform CPR already.

"After you, darling," I said, a Cheshire-cat grin ripening on my face.

Jen's flushed face twitched a meagre smile back at me as she entered the house, and I, chuckling softly, went in after her.

CHAPTER SEVEN

Jennifer

Talk about backfiring.

Never, ever could I have imagined the response that Henrik and Oonagh gave me on that doorstep. Still shaken from Wes' sudden move on me – which had left me light-headed and confused to say the least – they were the last thing I'd needed. Now I felt as if my head was on the verge of exploding, and they were going to add wine into the mix.

All right. I knew nothing about Wes' parents, and I had no right to expect that my "engagement ring" – in fact, a dastardly loan from Clara – would elicit the sort of reaction you'd get from, say, *my* brutal parents...but I still could never have predicted the applause I received instead.

Wes' parents resembled him in image only. His father, Henrik, looked like a Swedish architect with his tousled blond hair, gold-rimmed spectacles, and trim body in a roll-neck jumper and slimline jeans. Oonagh was beautiful in a witchy-way, with her sparkling green eyes outlined in thick black eye-liner, her hair salon-perfect in shades of plum and pillar-box red, rippling in waves to her shoulders. They had to be in their late sixties at least, but the air of youth and vitality surrounding them was palpable.

They looked like artists, and their home reflected the tastes and culture of well-travelled, well-cultured people. In the hall was a tall, wooden African sculpture of a mother with her two naked boys hugging her legs, while she balanced a basket of grain on her head. A nook beneath the stairs was taken up entirely by bookshelves, stuffed full of collected tomes from all over the world. At a glance I could see the spines of Ethiopian Cookery and Neolithic Pottery of the Philippines.

"Do you like reading, Jen?" asked Oonagh, seeing that I was interested in the books. "We collected so many books when Henrik and I were sent all over the world, bringing our surgical skills to rural communities."

"I love to read, when I get time," I said, carefully leaving out that I limited myself mostly to bodice-rippers as a way of unwinding and switching off. Though something told me that Oonagh wouldn't judge my tastes in fiction the way my own mother did. "What disciplines are you and Henrik in?"

"Actually I'm a cardiothoracic surgeon and Henrik is an orthopaedic surgeon. You'd be amazed at the issues we came across; some untreated for years and years in communities where they simply didn't have the technology to perform these surgeries," said Oonagh, taking a glass of white wine from Henrik.

He'd cracked open the bottle that Wes had brought with him – for some reason, that surprised me. My own parents would be dictating the wine list, telling their guests – including me – what they should want to drink.

He passed one to me, his blue eyes watching me closely.

"We had to have equipment shipped over. Some of our tools were stuffed into our suitcases. Do you remember when we gave the security people in Peru a run for their money?" Henrik chuckled as he tipped his glass to take a sip.

"Oh god, yes. They took everything out onto the table-tops and examined them one by one. The police were called. We had to be interviewed in separate rooms!" Oonagh creased up into a fit of giggles.

"Good times," said Henrik, shaking his head with a wistful grin on his face.

I found myself laughing, too. I glanced up at Wes and saw how relaxed he looked in the company of his mum and dad, jovially taking a sip of his wine as he laughed along with the story. A pang of jealousy rippled through me, taking me by surprise.

What really baffled me was their warmth; the overwhelming, welcoming, accepting aura that swept me away instantly. I felt like an empty cup being filled to the brim in one sudden movement with all the things my parents weren't. Until crossing their threshold, I hadn't realised just how much my relationship with my parents still bothered me these days. I thought I'd left all that in the past, before I'd finally qualified as a junior doctor and at least garnered some level of respect from them.

As I gazed up at the pieces of modern art above the fireplace and the glossy black grand piano in the dining room, another feeling crept its way in: guilt. I'd hoped to put a spanner in the works and give Wes a hard time, but it had backfired. Now I would have to keep up the act and allow these decent people to be deceived by a ring I didn't even own.

We took our wine to the table and continued talking back and forth, first about work and then exchanging stories. Mostly I deflected back to Wes or Oonagh, who were more than happy to hark back to travelling days, or stories of Wes' childhood. They'd run away to get married early in their career, taking Oonagh's surname for their married name. Henrik had disappeared to the back of the house to prepare the dinner, dipping in and out with a tea-towel slung over one shoulder.

"Wesley, do you remember when Dusty got into the barn at the house in Surrey, and you had to climb between all those bits of machinery just to get him?"

"God, yes," said Wes, his eyes glazing over as he remembered. "That wily little sod could get in just about anywhere."

"You must have heard about Dusty, Jennifer?" asked Oonagh, tilting her head to one side as she gave me an expectant glance.

"Of course," I said casually, remembering the photograph in Wes' office. "His sweet little dog with the shaggy grey fur."

"He once told his riding instructor that his scars were from a piece of machinery falling on his face," said Oonagh, winking at me. "He was always a sarcastic little thing."

"Serves him right for asking rude questions," said Wes.

"It's no wonder he went into craniofacial surgery. He was obsessed with making up stories about his face," said Oonagh. "Such a fixation on such a small thing."

"It was no small thing," said Wes, swallowing his wine with a hard gulp. "You try living with *bat face* from an early age."

"You had the sweetest little face," said Oonagh. "Even before the surgery. I've got thousands of photographs, Jen. It's really fascinating to see how he was before – "

"Please, mum, come on. Not at the dinner table," said Wes.

Hearing him speak of himself as something gross that shouldn't be discussed over dinner stabbed me a little in the heart. I shared a glance with Oonagh, whose eyes told me she felt the same way.

"I bet Jennifer would love to see your baby photos," said Oonagh. "Wouldn't you, Jen?"

"You bet I would," I said, finding myself genuinely interested. A little part of me that still wanted to give Wes some mischief sparked to life, urging me to beg for the baby photos, but I relented. I wasn't quite sure why. I wanted to teach him a lesson for having the audacity to kiss me and then ask me to pretend to be his girlfriend, didn't I?

"But...not if it makes Wes uncomfortable," I said, finally.

"I'm not uncomfortable," he said, frowning as he played with the stem of his glass. "I just think we should talk about something else."

"He's always done that, you know," said Oonagh. "Always had this thing about cups and glasses. He can't hold one without playing with it."

Henrik bustled through to the dining room, pushing a gold trolley stacked with a buffet of delicious meats, cheeses, pickles, and warm crusty breads. Together he and Oonagh dressed the table with dishes that smelled heavenly, including small crock pots of beef stew and a sizzling cheese fondue, with vegetables and breads for dipping. Once again, I was aghast at how casual and homely they were despite their obvious wealth. Never would my parents prepare food for *sharing* like this; and in any case, they'd have had housekeepers serving it.

Suddenly my stomach grumbled. I hadn't felt so ravenous in years. My eyes wandered over the tasty dishes, wondering where on earth to begin.

"Well, shall we start? Er, Jen – do you – that is – you aren't religious, are you?" asked Henrik, topping up my wine.

"We've no objections at all to saying grace before a meal, if that's what you like to do," said Oonagh with a gentle wink of one of her dazzling verdant eyes.

"Oh no, my parents were strictly atheist," I said. *And they certainly wouldn't have humoured anyone who wasn't like you would*, I wanted to add.

"But what about you, Jen?"

"Me?"

"Well, your parents aren't here," said

Oonagh, looking a little confused. I blushed furiously, realising I'd revealed in the clumsiest way just how attached I was to my parents, still considering myself to be an extension of them instead of my own person. What about *my* views on religion?

"Of course," I said, gulping hard. I realised that in all my years of studying and working towards one singular goal, I had never considered anything spiritual for myself. I had no idea what I thought of the world and the great beyond.

"I'm agnostic," I said eventually, shrugging my shoulders.

Henrik smiled a warm, gentle smile that put me at ease.

"Me too," he said softly.

"And me," said Wes, catching my eye. Finally, my tense shoulders were able to relax. Something about Wes' gentle support acted like a soothing balm.

"Well I'd like to say a few words," said Henrik, standing over the table with his glass raised. "Here's to meeting new friends. Here's to our son, Wesley – "

" – who never stops surprising us," said Oonagh with a smile toward me.

"And here's to the charming young woman before us, who we cannot wait to get to know, and who has so obviously made our son a very happy man," said Henrik. "Cheers to you, Jen!"

"Cheers!"

I downed my drink in one, wishing I could crawl under the table. I suddenly felt furious with Wes. How could he want to deceive these lovely, humble people? It would be one thing leading on *my* mum and dad, but to lie to Henrik and Oonagh, who clearly wouldn't hurt a fly, was too much to bear.

Suddenly the food didn't seem so appetising.

"Here, darling," said Wes, breaking me off a crust of hot steaming bread and serving me a spoonful of the stew. The savoury, delicious scent of it soon got my stomach working again. "Try some of this. My father makes this for every occasion."

I sighed and tucked in, finding that I cleared my plate with every new serving until I was warm and comfortably full. The food, at least, took my mind off the shame and guilt that was fast threatening to overthrow me. How could I have ever thought that I'd have fun doing this?

Once the meal was over, Wes helped Henrik clear the table, leaving me and Oonagh to chat. She asked me questions and endless follow-up questions about my work, my childhood, and my journey into plastics.

"You performed neonatal surgery?" asked Oonagh, gasping in astonishment. "Tell me all about that!"

As I told her, she nodded along, listening carefully and asking questions here and there. She seemed so genuinely mesmerised that I almost wanted to cry. As the conversation moved on and I felt heady and dreamy from the wine and good food, my eyes fell once more on the grand piano.

"Which of you plays the piano?" I asked.

Oonagh blinked. "You mean, you don't know?"

I shook my head, wondering what she was getting at. Then, too late, I remembered - Wes had played the piano at school. Oonagh looked concerned for a moment, then called out over her shoulder.

"Wesley, come here for a moment," she said. When Wes appeared, she stood, a pained expression increasing on her face. "Has Jennifer really never heard you play the *piano*?" She asked with an absurdity in her voice that made me flinch.

"We don't have many opportunities for that in the OR, mum," said Wes, looking sheepish all of a sudden.

"What rubbish! Get on that piano right now," said Oonagh, pointing her painted red nails towards it.

Henrik entered the room, wiping his hands on a kitchen towel. "What's the commotion?"

"She's never heard him play!"

Henrik blew out his cheeks and made a scoffing sound. "Get on the piano, Wesley!"

"Yes, Wesley," I said with a stiff voice. "*Get on the piano!*"

Wes made a grim smile and took a seat, looking suddenly at ease as his fingers caressed the keys. Once again I'd hoped to make him a little uncomfortable, only to be foiled by his coolness.

"Why don't you come and stand beside me, my love?" asked Wes, playing me at my own game. I almost wanted to grab a handful of his blonde locks and shake him by them, feeling violent as I was with guilt. This would only make it so much worse.

"I'm fine here, darling," I said through gritted teeth.

"Go and stand beside him," said Henrik in a whisper. "You won't regret it."

I rose, feeling a little wobbly as I made my way beside Wes. I turned and leaned a little against the piano to steady myself. I raised my eyebrows at him, communicating a message telepathically that I would damn-well get him for this.

"What have you got for me, Wes?" I asked.

"Hmm," he said, leaning back with his hand stroking his lightly stubbled chin. I was struck, once again, by how downright gorgeous he was, with his sculpted face and the jagged scar that fractured it. Seeing it now got me hot between my legs, making my thighs squirm a little as it sought to ease the aching.

"Something special," he said. "For you."

If he thought he was going to elicit some sort of gushing reaction from me, he was mistaken – no matter how fuckable he looked right now.

Wes' hands softly began to play, and my heart felt as if it was being squeezed when I recognised the tune.

His masculine hands with their long fingers teased out the opening notes to *Moon River*. My all-time favourite song. He couldn't possibly have known that. I'd never told anyone before.

Tears threatened to prickle my eyes, and I looked down at my hands on the gleaming black surface of the piano. I swallowed hard as the gentle, lullaby tune filtered in softly at first, before gradually filling the space of the room all around me with its gentle warmth.

I flinched as another sound joined the music. A gentle, deep, solemn voice began to sing the words. With a hint of naivety, his voice was uniquely beautiful.

Moon river, wider than a mile, I'm crossing you in style, someday.

My eyes found Wes, who looked sombrely at the keys as he played, glancing very briefly at me as his mouth formed the words. They seemed to come not from his mouth but from deep within him, beneath his diaphragm, yet were gentle and calming like a storm rumbling beyond distant hills. Powerful, and yet so peaceful.

Not only did he play like a concert pianist, but he sang professionally too – with just enough of that sibilance and slight impediment that made me giddy. This was Wes' rendition, especially for me. I felt that we were alone in the room, and I fought the urge to cry.

As the last tinkling notes faded out and Wes' parents applauded, I met Wes' gaze steadily, the longing between my legs threatening to implode me.

What are you doing? I wanted to ask him. *Why did you do this to me?*

Wes didn't seem able to tear his eyes off me, or I him. Something had to break the spell or else I could imagine us there forever, frozen in tableaux.

"Excuse me, I – " my voice was shaking, tears threatening to well up in my eyes. "There was a book in the hall I wanted to look at."

I heaved myself from the piano and hurried around the dining table and out into the hall, where the air was mercifully cooler.

"Why don't you give Jennifer a tour of the house?" I heard Oonagh ask. "We can get dessert ready in the meantime."

No, no, no. We couldn't be alone together. I didn't know what I'd do.

"Good idea," came Wes' deep voice.

Next I felt his warm hand on the small of my back, sending electrifying pulses throughout my body. My breaths came heavy as he guided me towards the stairs, taking my hand in his as we scaled them one by one. His hand held mine so firmly that I knew there'd be no escape; I'd never de-tangle myself from him now.

"This is the library," Wes said stiffly, swinging a large wooden door open very briefly, before pulling it shut again and moving us abruptly on. "This is the music room," he said, opening the door before pulling it shut seconds later. Never once did we actually step into the rooms. I felt dizzied, breathless. His clean scent at such close proximity made me want to bury my face in his clothes.

"This is the guest bedroom," he said, picking me up with both hands at my waist and whirling me inside. He slammed the door shut with a kick of his boot. It happened so quickly, I barely had a chance to let out a scream.

Suddenly his hands were all over me, caressing my hips, before trailing up my waist and cupping my breasts. My hands were in his hair and I groaned aloud with the sudden, painful aching that pulsed between my cleft, rippling up and through me, peaking at each nipple.

"Jen," he panted, making my love to my neck with his kisses, speaking breathlessly. "Tell me you're feeling this too?"

"Yes," I panted, tearing at the buckle on his belt – the one I'd wanted to whip from his pants all night. "God, yes."

In one swift movement, Wes scooped me up in his arms and carried me further into the room. I felt a cool bedspread beneath me, my body sinking into it as Wes leaned over me.

"Why?" I asked between gasps, his mouth finding mine in the dark. He kissed lazily, dragging his mouth over mine and laying kisses along my neck and jaw. "What were you thinking, playing that song to me?"

Wes cupped my jaw with his thumb and long fingers and drew my mouth close to his. I could feel his hot breath on my lips as he spoke in a close whisper. I couldn't see him at all in the pitch black room, but I could sense him, feel his muscular figure, all the same.

"What were *you* thinking, wearing that engagement ring?"

I paused my movements, realising my legs were tangled up in his. He had pinned me down to the bed, caging me with his strong arms.

I couldn't say what I really wanted to say, or ask what I wanted to ask. Namely: *why would you play that song to me, if this isn't real?*

Was he just getting his own back for my stunt with the ring, in the cruellest way possible?

"I was...I was just playing with you," I said finally, unsure, in truth, what to say.

Wes relaxed into me, his lips sinking against mine in a long, deep, grateful kiss. He pulled gently away to speak again. I could feel the length of him, his rock-hardness, against my thigh. He definitely wasn't playing pretend here – at least, not in the physical sense. That part was very real.

"Then I'd say we're even, wouldn't you?" he asked. "I can toy with you too, you see."

"Is that what you're doing right now?" I asked. My voice sounded weak with sincerity and I hated it; like a child, asking for affirmation. Yet, I needed to know.

"I haven't even begun," said Wes, nuzzling his nose against mine.

My fingers trailed up his arm and over his neck, searching for something I had felt with my lips. The darkness had fine-tuned my remaining senses, especially touch. There was another ridge on his lip that I had never seen with my eyes; a continuation of the deep scar that had adorned his austerely handsome face since childhood. It was distinctive in feel and texture against my lips, creating an imprint I would recognise in the darkness. My fingertips found his mouth and, without thinking, traced the edge of it.

Wes, to my surprise, placed a soft kiss on my fingertips. Panic leapt through my chest, then, realising I might have offended him. I stiffened in his embrace.

"Don't you like it?" he asked in a soft whisper.

Oh, quite the opposite. I had so many ideas for that ridge in that very moment, enjoying the way it protruded just slightly as we kissed.

"I think you know I do," I said, caving in to temptation.

I licked the ridge slowly; one soft lick that lead to a kiss on his top lip, before trailing small, slow kisses along the line of the scar, bending his head in my hands. With my palms flat either side of his head, I could feel the soft curl of his eyelashes against my thumb. He had closed his eyes to enjoy the sensations I gave him, and knowing that made my heart swell.

"What are you thinking of, when you touch my face like that?" he asked, his voice a hoarse whisper. His breaths tickled my skin.

I pressed my forehead to his, my fingertip still tracing the line of the scar beside his nose.

"I was imagining what that ridge would feel like if you pressed it between my legs," I said.

Wes let out a guttural moan, his hand

tugging up my skirt and lifting my leg aside. My arousal was so deep, pulsing within me, that I abandoned any formalities. We weren't doctors here. I wanted him to feel me.

With one open palm laid against my thigh, two fingers of his free hand gently eased my lace knickers aside and stroked between my labia. As he moved his hand to get a better position, his thumb nudged my clitoris, forcing out a weak moan of pleasure. So tender. So tight. He could bring my little aching bud to climax in moments.

"God, Jennifer, you're so wet. I haven't even done anything yet," he said.

I panted, my chest heaving with restrained longing. I wanted him to shove those two fingers deep inside me and see just how wet I could get.

"And you're so hard, like marble," I said, nudging the rock-hard bulge in his trousers with my knee.

Wes paused as if a thought had struck him, making me wait an agonising few seconds in his silence. He brought his lips to mine and kissed me, softly, before pulling my skirt back into place. I rolled my hips, aching for him to return and finish what he started.

"We can't do this here, beautiful," he said finally, from somewhere above me in the dark. "Not like this."

Now I was too worked up, and unable to

think straight. "Why the hell not?" I moaned, and felt his laughter in my hair as he pulled me closer to him once more. "*Why* did you stop?"

"Because we're in my parents' house, remember? And we're not two kids on summer break from college," said Wes. "I just couldn't keep my hands from you any longer, Jennifer, and I could tell you didn't want me to either."

I pressed a hand to his firm chest and pushed him up and away from me. This was the second time he'd done this to me; got me worked up, only to shatter the illusion. First the kiss in his office, and now this.

"What is this? It's like you're playing pretend with me. I'm your prototype girlfriend to experiment on."

"Jen, no. Absolutely not. It's me who can't believe his luck – "

"What are we doing here?" I hissed. "Because this all felt very real to me just now, and once again you're putting a stop to it." I was standing now, smoothing down my dress in the darkness. I felt along the wall until my fingers touched a light switch. On came the chandelier from the central ceiling rose, bathing us in harsh, cold light.

Wes looked rumpled but handsome, seated on the edge of the bed we'd occupied moments before. He blinked rapidly against the sudden brightness.

"I don't know what we're doing," said Wes, rubbing his face with his hands. "I think breaking up with you would do them more harm than good, even if it did assuage their fears of me being alone for a little while. They seem to love you already."

"Well we won't break up, because we aren't together," I said, making to pull off the faux-engagement ring. "We're colleagues, no more than that."

"What are you doing?" He looked up from his hands. "You can't take that off now."

"I'll tell them now. It'll make things easier than if we drag it out," I said, unsure where my sudden anger and determination had come from. Something about breaking that sexual spell had brought me some much-needed clarity.

"No! For god's sake, no." Wes rose from the bed and hurried to me, wiggling the diamond ring back down my finger. "You can't do that. Don't spoil this evening, Jen. For their sake, if not for ours."

"I'm not content with being used anymore," I said, struggling to breathe through the tightness in my chest. "I've decided I don't want to play this game."

"Jen," said Wes, holding me still by the shoulders, though I squirmed for release. "This is not a game, not to me. Not ever. I confess that I don't know what's happening between us...but please, you must believe me when I tell you that this was not planned."

"You're not *toying* with me then?"

"God, no. Not ever. I respect you, Jennifer. You are Dr Hurst before you're my intern, before you're my – whatever this is – "

"Girlfriend? Your idea, I might add."

"Fiance. Your idea." He folded his arms across his chest, his brow furrowing. "Let's just take a breather. We can have some dessert, say goodnight. I'll drive you back home, and we can figure out what to do about us later."

"You're not driving me home, Wes," I said. "I can get a cab. Besides, you've had too much wine to drive."

"I would insist on taking my fiancé right to her doorstep," said Wes in a firm tone of voice that made my skin prickle. "If we're to keep up this façade in the meantime, I *will* be escorting you home."

He paused, his head tilting as if considering something.

"By cab," he added finally.

"Fine," I said, placing my hand on the door knob. "But after tonight, I don't want to talk about this ever again. Not in work, and not outside of it. Got it?"

Wes closed his eyes slowly and nodded his

brief agreement. As I turned the door handle, Wes covered my hand with his.

"We'll go downstairs together," he said. "Make it look natural."

Sure, I thought. Natural. By some bizarre turn of events, it seemed to me that the only people so far who realised just how unnatural our coupling was, was us. As we descended the stairs, I cringed at the ways I'd allowed myself to respond to him, to be swept away by him, bending instantly to his will when he summoned me, as if calling to a canary high up in a tree. Down I'd fluttered.

And all it had taken was one beautiful, sweet song.

CHAPTER EIGHT

Wesley

We were due to meet our new patient in 15 minutes and Jen was still pacing back and forth in the break room, her head glued to that bloody phone of hers. It pained me to see her, knowing how soft and right she felt in my arms. Knowing that she wouldn't let me experience the bliss of that ever again, not now that I'd offended her.

I'd only wanted to be with her somewhere private, somewhere special. But none of that mattered now.

I sipped my hot tea and glanced down again at the patient schedule for the day, though I'd waited so long that I knew the day's rota by heart now. If Jen even so much as threatened to make us late for the meeting, I was going to storm in there, grab her phone, and toss it down the sluice chute.

Janine, with her back to me, was scribbling

the schedule on the whiteboard. The night shift nursing staff were scooting around and by me, finishing up before the handover. I stayed firm, rooted to my spot, sipping my tea with my eyes fixed on the break room door.

"She's stopped pacing now," I muttered. "I can't see her roaming back and forth in front of that pane of glass anymore."

"Hm?"

"Do you suppose she's ended the call?"

"What? What were you saying, Dr Brookes?"

I scoffed under my breath. "Who the hell would she be having a serious conversation with at this hour, right before morning clinic starts?"

In my periphery, I saw Janine glance toward the break room and dramatically roll her eyes, the whites of them glistening.

"Maybe someone died," she said gruffly.

I stiffened, my hand curling tight around the handle of my mug of tea. Maybe she was right. Maybe Jen was in pain, suffering, and I was standing around out here, doing nothing about it.

"She didn't say anything to you about any sick family members, did she?"

Janine groaned aloud. "No, she didn't. But if you want to know so badly, why don't you go in there and ask her? You're her boss."

I swallowed a gulp of tea and slammed the

mug down on the top of the nurses' station.

"You know what? You're bloody-well right," I said, wiping my mouth on the back of my wrist. I bowled my way to the break room, barely registering Janine's voice calling after me, asking something about the Saturday dinner.

How had it gone – was she asking that? Disastrously. Wonderfully. I didn't fucking know anymore.

To plan, I supposed. That was one way of putting it.

My parents had been thrilled to meet the new "love" in my life. I'd slept easier that night than I'd slept in years in my quiet, very still apartment. The knowledge that, for once, they weren't fretting over my mental health since the incident with Rebecca and Theo, had given me a brief serenity that would see me through the week.

If only I hadn't upset Jen so much.

Well, she *had* pulled that stunt with the diamond ring – but nevertheless, Jen had been doing me a favour, and it was fast leading to more trouble for the both of us than it would be worth.

Why, then, did it still feel so very, very right, in spite of our misunderstanding?

I elbowed the door open and found myself surrounded by stillness. Craning my neck and peering around the room, the eeriness spooked me. I wasn't the most perceptive chap at the best of times, and yet I could feel something was wrong with Jen, as if the world was off its axis. Frowning, I took off my surgical cap and let my scalp breathe, running a hand through my hair as I made for the bunk room.

As I gingerly opened the door, I heard the soft, snuffly sounds of Jen crying. She was there, crouched on the floor between two beds with her back against the far wall. Her knees were drawn up to her chin, with her face creased in a painful sob against her knuckles.

I felt an instant need to go to her, to gather her up in my arms – but I couldn't. I'd already confused her enough, and she'd made it clear she was through with me. My role now was to be her mentor and do what was best for her – and that meant keeping my hands off.

I let the door softly close behind me and joined her on the ground, crouching down before her small, crumpled form.

"Jen? Jen, what is it?"

She shook her head in despair, grinding her knuckles into the space between her eyes.

"Just give me a minute," she said in a whisper.

"You're in no state to see our patient in clinic this morning," I said gravely. "Not unless you can snap out of this quick as a wink."

Jen wiped her face and let out a long breath.

"Fuck, I forgot – I can't believe I forgot. I thought we had a free morning."

"That's tomorrow," I said. "We never have a free morning on Mondays."

"Right, right," said Jen, smoothing down her ponytail.

"I think we could solve this a lot faster if you just told me what the problem is," I said. I drew in a low breath. "It's not...it's not about Saturday, is it?"

"God, no," said Jen, wiping her nose. I took a clean handkerchief from my scrubs pocket and gave it to her. She gave a small, grateful smile as she dabbed her nose and face.

"You can have that one on me," I said.

Jen laughed involuntarily through her tears. I was glad I could at least do that for her.

"Now tell me," I said.

She gulped hard and sighed. "My parents finally caught wind of the fact that I moved from the neonatal unit into plastics."

"You never told them?"

"God, no. My mum called. She just wanted to tell me what a disappointment I am, and to ask why it was that she couldn't trust me with the simple task of completing the programme in the discipline I chose. She said a whole heap of stuff."

I should have been angered by their lack of faith – not to mention their interference – with Jen and her decision-making. And I was, deeply so. But I also couldn't help feel a spark of familiarity, to see someone as hung up about their own parents as I was. Keeping my parents happy had been the sole reason for our pact, after all. I understood the need for parental approval on a bone-deep level.

"You want them to be proud of you," I said.

"Of course I do," said Jen. "But a pig will be performing face-lifts before that ever happens."

"Why didn't you ask for their blessing, if it matters that much to you?"

"Should I have to?" asked Jen, her voice sounding child-like in a way that pulled on my heart. "Besides, what incentive do I have to tell them *anything* about me when they overreact like this?"

"It...it hurts to see you like this," I said in a whisper. "I wish you'd let me hold you."

Jen looked at me, then, square in the eyes. Her eyes followed the strands of my hair from my scalp to where they fell by my cheekbones. I knew she was admiring me, and it felt too good. The way she regarded me like something Michelangelo had created sent my ego sky-high, unreservedly so, and it was all I could do not to repay her in kind.

"You'd hold me? Here?"

"I'd hold you anywhere," I said, letting a laugh escape my lips as all my pent-up emotion threatened to burst out of me like a breaking dam.

"I've thought of nothing else since Saturday."

She looked exhausted, fragile. I knew that if I could just hold her, let my ever-growing feelings for her seep from me and into her, I could give her what she needed. She would absorb me like a drug and feel some of the headiness I was feeling. I would cocoon her in my reverence until she felt it to her core, and believed it.

"Me either," she said weakly. "Despite everything I said, it's all I think about. It's all I want to think about."

A beeping sound interrupted us. It was my pager, telling me we had five minutes. I silenced it, cursing under my breath. There never seemed to be enough time.

"To hell with it," I said.

Before she could object, I curled one arm under Jen's legs and the other beneath her shoulder blades, lifting her to the bottom bunk with me. I held her small figure in my lap and squeezed her, knowing that endorphins would be flooding her, sending signals all around her body that she was safe, protected. Understood. She sank into my arms, quivering.

A terrible memory resurfaced from my school-days as I held her.

I was hiding in the cloak room, praying I wouldn't be found. I could hear their chants echoing from somewhere down the long, ghostly halls of our boarding school. *Bat-face, bat-face, bat-face*. Then my father, appearing long after the other boys had been picked up for the half-term break, roaming between the coat-racks. Then his arms around me, holding me tight as he could, until I found the strength to get up and walk with him out into the courtyard where our car was parked.

No words were exchanged; his understanding was evident when he held me, going right to the source of the pain.

Jen went limp in my arms, her head burrowed into my neck.

"You belong here, Jen. You belong here with me. You bring value to me and to our patients. Don't you ever doubt it. I'm *glad* you moved into plastics," I said, keeping my voice earnest and clear, so there could be no confusion.

Jen lifted her head and faced me, already looking soothed and more relaxed, if a little defeated.

"You won't be saying that when I tell you the rest," she said in a hopeless tone.

I blinked. "What do you mean? What else do you have to tell me?"

"I told you my parents are surgeons too, right?"

"Yes."

"Well they've heard through the grapevine that a certain retired orthopaedic surgeon met his wonderful new daughter-in-law-to-be on Saturday. She works in plastics with his son. He even named her," said Jen, shaking her head solemnly. "So as well as declaring me a disgrace for my career choices – which they learned about through gossip – they've also declared me a disgrace for getting engaged without telling them, too."

I paused for a few moments, letting the news sink in.

"I see."

"And now they've demanded to meet you. Tonight. No excuses."

Now it was my turn to feel uncomfortable, frozen with indecision. There was no way I could let her down – not after she'd held up her end of the deal – but this was fast getting out of hand.

"Why didn't you tell them it wasn't true? That it's a harmless ruse?"

"Right, because that'd be even better – I'd look *really* impressive to them then," said Jen, levering herself out of my arms. I was glad that she at least had the strength to pull away from me and stand by herself. That was progress. She sniffed, wiping the tears from her face. She turned to look at me. "You owe me this. You're doing it."

I raked my hands through my hair, feeling

a fool. I should have known my parents would be so elated about my engagement that they'd tell all and sundry. I'd become so wrapped up in my growing feelings for Jennifer that I'd forgotten to ask them to keep it quiet.

"This is becoming a nightmare," I said. What the hell had possessed me to do this in the first place?

I knew, deep down, exactly why. I'd been giving it a lot of thought.

It was Jen. I needed her. I wanted her. But I couldn't trust her any more than I could trust any woman, not ever again, and so I'd created a controlled environment. A comfortable fantasy where I could pretend for a little while.

Only it was fast spiralling out of my control and into the hands of anyone who wanted to stick their oar in. The more people got involved, the harder it would be to keep a lid on things. It was, potentially, already far too late. We'd be the talk of the department in no time.

"What's the matter? Afraid that my parents won't fall head over heels for you, the way yours did for me?"

I narrowed my eyes at her. "Not at all."

"Then do it. Tonight."

"I'm afraid my schedule won't allow – " I began desperately, but Jen was having none of it.

"Screw you, Wes. You owe me this, so you're damn-well doing it, or I'll – "

She faltered. I took full advantage.

"Or you'll what, Jen?"

She looked so beautiful with her tear-stained face, highlighting her nose and cheeks with a sweet, youthful pink aspect.

"Or I'll be going straight back to neonates and you'll never see me set foot in this ward again," she said, in a steely tone.

"Now that would be a shame," I said honestly. "And it would be a decision you would regret."

"It's a decision I'll make, Wes. Now it's time you made yours. I'll forward *you* the details."

Jen washed her hands in the basin by the door, before splashing her face and patting it dry with a blue paper towel. She didn't wear even the slightest brush of powder or rouge, giving her a pure, honest appearance, like an angel.

Bizarre longings came over me as I watched her adjust herself in the mirror's reflection. How could I tell her that she needn't do anything – that she looked like perfection incarnate? I wanted to roll my tongue over her pure white skin, tasting her. Her beautiful, unblemished skin.

"Be there, Dr Brookes. I'm not kidding," she said, pulling open the bunk room door by its metal handle. Artificial light flooded in like spilled juice across the floor. "I'll see you in the clinic. They're waiting for us."

I watched Jen walk away, with her delectable buttocks tucked neatly into her tight black work trousers, swaying as she picked up her pace. She thought she was winning something, but I'd brought her back from her hopelessness. Me.

I was winning.

And the pleasure was still – despite whatever may await me later – all mine.

CHAPTER NINE

Jennifer

I rushed from the tree-lined entrance to Sacred Heart and made the bus with seconds to spare. I pressed my phone against the reader just as the bus lurched to life and pulled away. Sighing, I held tight to the railings as I found myself a seat. My shoulders were weighted down by the albatross I'd carried ever since that awful phone call from Alison, with my father throwing in the odd cluck of disgust from the background.

I'd disappointed them in multiple ways. Again. What was new?

As I watched the darkness fall down over the glowing street lamps, I wondered why I still cared when I'd promised myself years ago – more than a decade ago, even – that I'd leave them both in the past just as soon as I began studying medicine. That once I'd fulfilled my obligation and spared them the embarrassment of becoming anything but a doctor, I'd tell them both to go eat shit.

Yet here I was, still taking their phone calls, still doing as I was told. Despite living in my own flat-share and throwing myself into my career, they lingered still above my shoulder, whispering their chiding, seething remarks in my waiting ear.

I sighed, putting in my ear buds to listen to a podcast. Without the benchmark of those remarks I so loathed, I was lost, drifting, unable to replace their opinion of me with one of my own. It was my fault. I'd never developed the ability to seed my own self-assurance.

And to make matters worse, here I was, on my way to snag a new dress from a coat-rail in a nauseatingly-expensive boutique for a dinner party with these people. No, worse still – I was dragging Wes into it. I almost felt guilty, knowing they'd rake him over the same coals they'd been stoking since I was born, punishing him for his connection to me. How could I knowingly do that to him, a man I so admired – the man who was to teach me everything?

As the anxiety rose like bile up my throat and settled painfully in my chest, I called Clara and explained the situation.

"Why are you so worried about him? Didn't he start this whole thing in the first place?"

"Yes, technically it's his damn fault my parents found out about us, but I'm just as much to blame. What's that phrase? You play stupid games, win stupid prizes? Well this is my stupid prize."

"And his, too. Maybe now he'll see it isn't okay to use people as handy props. Next he'll be getting you to bring his schedule and make his tea like that charge nurse of his," said Clara. "He's fucking her, you know that, right?"

I held my tongue, knowing I'd thought the same thing – but Wes seemed too different, too...indescribably awkward, actually, to be into casual flings. He'd held off from me even when I'd been hot and ready for him, leaving me dismayed at his self-control. I told Clara as much and was rewarded with her scoffing laughter reverberating against my eardrum.

"He's a man – that's all I'm saying."

"And what if I told you I'd opened up like a damn flower, inviting him to – " I glanced around at the packed bus. " – Pollinate me – and he'd had the self-restraint to pull back and stop?"

Clara was silent for a moment. "I'd say he must be gay," she said, making me laugh. "No, really. It's weird, all this starting and stopping. Does he want you, or not?"

"My thoughts exactly," I said. "At this point, I don't care. I just want to get through this gruelling dinner, come up with some excuse for our faux-break-up in a few weeks, and go back to my miserable life."

"Your life is not miserable, sweetie. Your life is just beginning. He's the arsehole for picking on his own intern, testing and tasting you at his own leisure. He should be ashamed of himself."

That was the problem. I wanted him to pick on me. I wanted him to *pick me*.

As I hopped off the bus and began my languid searching through the skimpy clothes racks, with their expensive scraps of material that they called dresses, one of my mother's scathing remarks entered my head.

You want to be an intern for ever, is that it? More comfortable being the underling, the student, when you should be a leader by now?

That was the remark that had me crouching on the ground, hugging my own knees as I cried. My mother, genius-bitch that she was, had a way of hitting the nail on the head.

And whose fault is that? I'd wanted to scream down the phone at her. *Who made me this way, afraid of standing on my own two feet?*

"And I'm the loser still blaming her parents for all her problems when she's over thirty years old," I said, muttering bitterly under my breath.

Was it any wonder that my knees liquefied at the sight of Wes' strong shoulders, the thick veins in muscular arms that promised a tight, safe embrace? Was it any wonder that it should be Wes who awoke those feelings in me – my teacher, my leader – a man so senior to me in age and experience?

"A thirty-year-old with a daddy-crush on her boss," I said quietly to myself. "How original."

I clucked my tongue at my own lack of class as I held up the perfect dress to the light. It was black, classic, with an edgy cross-body, one-shoulder affair that would match the stark modern art in my parents' apartment. I'd look like one of their lamps, or perhaps a chic vase. They'd approve of it.

But it wasn't actually their approval I was craving, not tonight. It was Wes'.

Ever since that song, that moment in the bedroom, that embrace in the bunk room –

It would always be his I was searching for.

♥

He was there, as promised. Wes's cab was parked right outside my mum and dad's apartment building.

Colossally tall, black and severe, looming over the street like the Death Star – I couldn't imagine who on earth would want to build such a hideous piece of architecture. I'd always considered this place my mum and dad's own perverse Xanadu; a place most people would stagger from in revulsion, sensing its malevolence like an ancient ghost. My parents revelled in it. They belonged there. It was their dark tower, and

123

the place they intended to retire in.

Hardly a quaint bungalow in the Cotswolds.

I heard the car door slam and felt him standing by me. His presence turned my gaze from the building I so feared. He had one hand in his pocket, and the other holding the neck of another bottle of wine.

Wes took my breath away quite literally as he stepped into the warm glow of light from the foyer. So tall and delicious, with his emerald eyes catching the light. He wore a simple pair of dark grey trousers and a black shirt, no tie, which clung to the toned, hard body beneath it.

So simple and elegant, with his hair gently tousled and effortlessly sexy. The way the shadows played on his eyes as he walked towards me gave him a brooding darkness that I wanted to melt into. The light from the foyer highlighted the ridges of his facial scar, finishing at his lip where my eyes were drawn to the very spot I longed to kiss.

A holy desire for him turned away in my womb, reaching its fingers down into my clit, spreading inside me. Wesley Brookes. How I wanted him. How I wanted him to want me.

"Jennifer," he said, in that stern parental tone that made me breathless. Disbelief misted over his expression as he took me in, his astute gaze lingering, judging me. He made me fearful of his assessment of me, and yet desperate for it, too.

"How do you shift between two states like that, so seamlessly?" he asked, his voice trailing away as the words left his mouth. "How are you a child one moment, and the next..."

"The next, what?" I asked.

"The next...so severe in your beauty as to terrify me," he said. "You could devastate any man and you don't even know it, do you?"

I laughed, then. "Wes, you're embarrassing me."

"I'm telling you the truth. If you want to reach your potential as a surgeon, Jen, you'd better start accepting who you are."

I don't know who I am, I thought immediately.

I felt pathetic already, knowing that Wes could see right through me; knowing that being this dangerously close to co-dependency is what had kept me single.

"Listen, this isn't going to be comfortable, or fun, or pleasant in any way. I'd spare them your fawning of me – they won't want to hear it. They certainly won't believe it," I said, hugging my arms around my waist.

Concern etched Wes' brow as he approached me. I lowered my head and looked at a paving slab on the ground, focusing on a piece of chewing gum. Anything but meet his gaze. Wes reached out and hooked his finger under my chin, tilting my head up to look at him.

"I'll make them hear it," he said firmly, as if in solemn promise. The hairs on my bare arms stood on end, my skin shivering in the chill night air. Something about his eyes spoke of honesty, integrity; the promise of a good doctor. I found myself believing him.

"Okay," I said in a whisper.

He let his hand fall from my chin and cupped it over my shoulder. The warmth of his palm seeped through me, making me feel like I was sinking into a warm bath.

"We can do this. Put your trust in me," he said. His hand dropped once more from my shoulder and found my hand, lacing his fingers in mine. Warm, reassuring, strong. I found the courage from his touch to enter the building and speak to the front desk, telling them that guests of David and Alison Hurst had arrived.

As we waited for the lift to arrive, I realised my fingers were still laced with Wes'. He had a kind of determined air about him, with all his usual awkwardness absent. Something had changed. I found myself flattered, sensing that he was ready to show himself and dare them to criticise him the way they criticised me, knowing it would be impossible.

He was Wes Brookes. They would *know* his name; know the depth of experience and reverence that supported his status.

A transparent orb of safety surrounded us, totally impenetrable. I felt strong beside him, as if he completed a void in me that my parents would probe if only they could break our protective spell.

I was ready to face them.

I rapped on the double doors to my parents' penthouse apartment, my strength renewed. They would deplete it, I was sure, over the course of the evening. They always did. But with Wes by my side, I knew I could withstand it.

A pang of sadness rippled through me as I remembered a key fact: Wes was not my fiancé. We weren't even a couple. None of his strength really belonged to me at all.

The door opened in that moment, revealing a member of mum and dad's household staff.

The woman, wearing a black top and trousers and a solemn expression to match, showed us into the grand living room. I took in the sight of the enormous black marble fireplace and long sectional white sofas. My mother lounged with a glass of wine, watching the blue flames licking inside it. My father, resting in his wheelchair, was reading a book. They couldn't have looked less like they were expecting us, content to appear nonchalant, even cold. The contrast between my parents and Wes' was already staggering.

"Ah," said dad, peering over the rim of his transparent specs. "They're here, Alison."

"Mm?" My mother glanced lazily from the fire and saw us, rising from her chair with her eyes fixed on Wes. My mother was lean and elegant, with long greying blonde hair that she had pinned up in a severe bun. She was beautiful in a stark way; like me, but with sharper edges and a meanness in her eyes, more grey in colour than blue like mine.

She went to Wes first, reaching out her hand to shake his. Her eyes didn't even so much as wander to me.

"Dr Brookes. It's a pleasure to meet you," she said, looking reluctantly impressed by Wes. There was, at least, some professional respect there.

Dad balanced his book on his thigh and wheeled his way over, wincing as he did so. He'd been suffering with arthritis for the last year or so, preventing him from performing surgeries. I'd heard via my mother's dreadful phone calls that he'd struggled to adjust to his declining health and that, frankly, so had she.

He reached out and shook Wes' hand firmly despite the pain it must have caused him, betraying none of it in his expression.

"Good to meet you, Dr Brookes."

"I'll take that," said my mother, turning the bottle of wine in her hands with an arched eyebrow. My father led the way to the grand dining room, furnished with a sleek, black, glass table and starkly white, modern, high-backed chairs which contrasted against it.

The silence among us was deafening, making me dizzy as the blood drummed in my ears. I held tight to Wes' arm, wishing he and I could be anywhere but here. If his family home had been a hive of warmth and love, then this was a desolate place, with a vacuum where love should be.

We sat. Wes and my parents did the perfunctory sharing of disciplines and a brief run-down of their career paths. My mother – who still hadn't made any eye contact with me, and nor had my father, for that matter – detailed her career in ophthalmic surgery, while my father detailed his career in nephrology.

"We had hoped Jennifer would become a neonatal surgeon. Ever since she was a little girl, she was obsessed with babies - naturally, we encouraged her down that pathway," said my mother, her lips thinning as she grimaced. "What a pity."

"We can only guide our children as best we can," said my dad, swilling his wine in the glass. "If they will insist on sabotaging their own progress, what can one do?"

I winced, looking down at my lap. I'd been waiting for this. What I didn't have the courage to say was that I had only gone into neonatal surgery to make them happy. Moving to plastics after I'd completed my first year of interning was the first career choice I'd ever made on my own.

And I hadn't regretted it, not for a moment. I never would. We shared a horrible silence, filled with all the things I couldn't say.

Meanwhile, silent members of housekeeping brought in trays of cold, fresh sushi – though the fish looked to me like a sickly jelly, and the rice stodgy and unappealing. I could imagine any one of those sushi rolls getting stuck in my throat, and I realised with horror that I would rather that than to continue eating this dry, loveless dinner around a table of pure malice.

Only when my mother finally allowed her gaze to drift to me did they cut right to the chase.

"Now, tell me, Dr Brookes – David and I are simply dying to know. As a consultant, what ethical quandaries did you bypass in order to engage in a relationship with our daughter?"

I choked on my wine, spluttering over the single sushi roll on my otherwise barren plate.

Wes let his left hand wander discretely behind my back, rubbing in slow circles between my shoulder blades. With his right hand, he passed me a linen napkin. When I glanced up at him between coughs, I noticed that his eyes never left my mother. Their emerald beauty had been replaced with a cold, steely determination that I'd only seen before in the OR.

"I'm delighted to tell you that there were no ethical quandaries, in that case. Though Jen is my intern, she's also a colleague, a peer. I've breached no duty of care to her in that sense."

"Really? That's interesting," said my father, looking genuinely interested, but only in that psychopathic way of his. With his almost entirely bald head and cold, grey eyes behind his glasses, he studied Wes, his eyes narrowing to slits. It was as if he was trying to comprehend the incomprehensible. "Well I have to say that I think most consultants would disagree with that view, Wesley."

My mother snorted, lacking my father's passive aggression – with her, it was always direct.

"You don't consider the obvious power imbalance to be an issue? Jen is barely out of university. You're a seasoned surgeon in your...what is it? Late thirties, forties?" said my mother.

"I'm well out of university – " I tried, but my small voice wouldn't carry. I wanted to scream, to flip the table, but I knew that even if I did that, they still wouldn't hear me.

"Again, with respect, Jennifer is a qualified doctor who has already demonstrated her skills. First in the neonatal unit, and now to me in plastics. She's fast on her way to becoming a surgeon in her own right," said Wes. The earnest tone of his masculine voice made me want to throw my arms around him. I could tell he meant what he said.

This time, my father dropped the reserved act and joined my mother in a cruel chortle.

"You wouldn't be biased about that, would you, Dr Brookes?"

"Please," said my mother. "You're taking advantage. And you, Jennifer – well, you – "

"Disappoint you," I said flatly, taking a sip of my tasteless wine. It was the very same wine that Wes had brought to his parents' house, and it had tasted beautiful there. In this apartment, it was void of any flavour at all. "I know."

My mother looked at me incredulously, as if wondering where I'd got my sudden balls from – and the truth was, I didn't know. With Wes' support and belief in me, I was finding my own courage.

"I perfected my own bone graft the other day, mother. It was a beauty. I wish you could have seen it," I said.

"You've always been gifted, Jennifer. We've

said as much. But what a shame you've decided to throw away any credibility you might have built by jumping departments and taking up with your superior," said my father in a low, reprimanding tone.

"*Very* unfortunate," said my mother, with thin lips that pursed as she eyed my small form.

I shrank in my seat, bowing my head. I was five again, crying as I struggled to lace my shoes in the precise way my mother had shown me. Long, intricate laces on high Victorian-style boots. In my mind's eye I could see my nanny, Eva, beside me. Covering her mouth in despair at the ways my own mother tormented me, helpless to defend me against her.

I swallowed another gulp of wine, feeling nauseas as it went straight to my head. A boldness came over me as I remembered that little girl, her tear drops falling on the white leather of the shoes I'd so hated.

"Let's face it. You were never going to respect any man who respected *me*," I said. Rage pulsed through my veins with explosive intent. How – how could they invite him in and attack him like this? They could go for me – they were used to doing that. But him? I couldn't stand it.

"Now, now, Jennifer. There's no need to get emotional," said my father.

My mother laughed cruelly. "Rational as

always," she said, rolling her eyes.

I stood up, tears welling in my eyes despite all my efforts to shove emotion to the back of my mind. It was a feat just to do that. I didn't want to give them the satisfaction of seeing it – not ever – but I wasn't made of stone either.

"Wes has been recognised across the world for his designs and developments. Even you must have heard of the Brookes Bolt, the multi-way mechanical fixing for bone grafts? It was pretty fucking pioneering. But the moment he's associated with me, you see fit to dismiss him – "

Wes stood up with me, a comforting hand on my hip.

"Darling, you're far too flattering – " he began, then made to nuzzle my ear. As his lips brushed the shell of my ear as he whispered, "Don't give in to them. Be strong."

But I didn't feel strong – I couldn't be strong. Not around them. Not ever. This evening had well reminded me of that fact.

"I think the alcohol has gone to her head, poor lamb," said my mother.

"You really should learn restraint," said my father.

I threw down my napkin.

My parents' eyes fixed on the napkin as if I'd just laid down a grenade.

Wes cleared his throat, never letting his hand leave my waist. He was doing a very good job of pretending to be my fiancé, I had to admit. In fact we hadn't struggled with our *act* for even a moment. I realised in that moment, in contrast to how afraid of him I'd been on my first day, that I felt at home with Wes now. He had become my guardian, my protector, and my safe place.

But was that merely a result of proximity, intimate surgeries, his coaching...or something else truly blossoming between us? The same thing which made Wes, who was by all accounts a stuck-up grouch with an attitude problem, into this comforting romantic? This lover who couldn't keep his fingertips from tracing patterns on my skin?

I glanced up at him. My tear-filled eyes met his cool, confidant, reassuring ones.

"Let's get out of here, Wes," I said.

"You've got it," he said, smiling gently down at me. He turned to face my parents, still seated, whose eyes went from the unexploded napkin up to him as if pulled by a fishing wire. "It was a pleasure to meet you both."

"And you, Dr Brookes," said mum.

"Likewise," said my dad.

I fisted my hands at my sides and stormed from the room, feeling coiled, stiff, gritting my teeth. Wes kept his hand on the small of my back, guiding me through the stark, foreboding apartment to the front door. In their hallway I stopped dead, seeing the solemn photograph of me in its frame. A pale young woman with a lank ponytail and a half-smile, her eyes dead as a fish on ice.

Humiliated. Rejected. I could handle that – I'd expected that – but to target Wes? My awkward, yet considerate mentor?

Who the hell did they think they were?

My hand flung out to grab the photo frame and, in one vicious movement, I threw it down on the cold tiled floor of the hall. The glass shattered at my feet with a satisfying smash. I stood over it, shivering, enjoying how the light glinted on the specks of glass. I felt Wes' lips in my hair, kissing the back of my head. I closed my eyes and thought of that ridge on his lips, the sexy scar that I wanted to trace with my tongue. My heart beat faster.

Once outside, Wes insisted on calling me a cab and escorting me to my front door. We took the ride in silence, and when he walked me up the steps to my place, he paused. Agitation rippled the frown line between his eyebrows.

"I – Jen, I need to apologise to you." He sighed, bowing his head. "This has been a dreadful idea from the very start. Now that it's impacting your life personally, I can see what a selfish arse I was to ever ask this of you."

"You couldn't have known. Your parents are darlings. They'll never be disappointed in you," I said, sighing. "I blame myself. I agreed to it so I could mess with you a little."

He looked up. "Why would you want to mess with me?"

"Because of the kiss," I said, colour flooding my face as I remembered it. I'd suppressed a crush on Wes, misunderstood him, and revealed myself. It wasn't his fault – and yet it was. It was, it was, it was. "You made me reveal my feelings about you in your office, like an idiot. Then there's what happened in the guest bedroom."

Confusion crossed Wes' face. The moonlight picked out the greens and yellows of his eyes, making my heart pound.

"You think I didn't like it, when we first kissed?"

"You said as much, didn't you?"

"Jen, I thought – " He paused, frowning as he tried to conjure up the correct words. I waited, knowing Wes enough by now to know that he needed patience. "Didn't I speak with my response to you, with my hands and my mouth, and my – for god's sake, Jen, later, in the guest bedroom of my parents' house! How could you think I don't want you?"

I flinched at those words – *want you*. That

137

was all I was aching for – for Wes Brookes to want me. To really want me. To need me, like I needed him.

"We were playing pretend. Caught up in the moment," I said meekly. I decided I would ask something that had been playing on my mind, driving me crazy. "That song you sang to me – was it really for me, or just for show?"

He winced, bowing his head and shaking it.

"I chose that song because you embody it, and it came to mind as easily as that," he said, looking back up. "I only had to look at you. If you were a sound, a song – it would be that one. Soft, elegant, hopeful, ambitious, dreaming – "

Impassioned suddenly and about to lose my mind, I grabbed Wes, holding him either side of his breathtakingly handsome face. He stopped mid-sentence, making a sound as if air had caught in his throat. Then desire made its hazy impression on his features and he closed his eyes as I kissed him, hungrily. If he wanted to speak to me with body language, then he needn't say any more. I could show him.

"God, *Jennifer*," he said when I yanked his body against mine, my back against the door, my arms entwining his neck. With a handful of his hair in each hand, I slammed my open mouth against his, devouring him. As his desire made itself known against my navel – long, rigid, and pulsing – he groaned and pawed me, kissing me back long and deep and with as much desperation as I had shown him.

His hands roamed my body through the thin silk material of my dress, his thumb and forefinger seeking my nipples. He found them, erect enough to cut glass, and began to pinch and roll them as he moaned inside my mouth.

When we came up for air, he pressed his forehead to mine, seemingly lost in lust and tormented by something else. His face twisted in pain as he caged me against the door, smothering me in his scent of sex and desire, cocooning me in him.

"Why did you let me do this to you – to make you pretend? Why did you let me use you when it was so wrong?"

I drew on his bottom lip, sucking it and grazing it gently with my teeth. His erection pulsed deliciously, so I did it again.

"Don't you know?"

"You say you wanted to mess with me, but when you arrived you were stunning, achingly sexy. You were the perfect guest. Polite, interested. You responded to me. You knew what you were doing," said Wes, panting. I pawed his abdomen and ran kisses along his jaw as he spoke.

"I wanted to be used by you," I said.

Our eyes met. A dark desire pooled in his

eyes like a storm, and he grunted, lifting me up off the ground with an arm under each thigh so my legs could encircle his waist.

My skirt shifted obscenely high, revealing where my stockings met my suspenders. Now his cock was ludicrously straining in his pants, making me squirm as its hot beating column nestled against my cleft. The pulsing bud of my clitoris sent a shudder through me as I began to grind my hips, rolling his heavy shaft against it. With his arms beneath my thighs, his hands cupped my taught buttocks, his fingers probing the molten passage between.

"Jen," he groaned, kissing the line of my jaw with a lazy open mouth, his teeth clenching down on my chin, trailing soft bites down my neck.

"My bed," I gasped. "Take me to my bed right now."

"Agh, stop," he said in a pained, reluctant grunt. "Stop, stop."

"What? *Why*?"

Wes lowered me, smoothing down my dress and my hair. I was quivering, too foggy brained to properly stand. His warm hands soothed me, holding me under my jaw as he planted soft, apologetic kisses on my forehead.

"You live in this house with how many other people?"

I groaned impatiently.

"Four," I said, sounding like a spoiled brat who'd been denied a cookie. No, not a cookie. Access to the damn bakery.

"If I'm taking you, Jen, I want you to be all mine. I don't want to share your beautiful sighs and screams with a house full of people."

I knew I couldn't care less who heard. When I was as hot for him as this, all my inhibitions – and common decency, in fact – went right out the window. I would come loudly for all the street to hear for all I cared, as long as it was him between my legs.

"I don't care about that," I said, pressing my lips to his. "I need you to show me you want me, Wes. This isn't a joke. Show me that those shit excuses for parents are wrong about me. Show me your regard for me with your body. Fuck me until I can be under no illusions!"

"I will, angel. Tomorrow night, after work. Let me show you my home; let me treat you with the respect you deserve, in a space that can be ours all night." Wes kissed me softly, sensually, promising me with his lips. His hand slipped under my skirt, his two fingers beckoning against my hungry, unsated clit. I moaned inside his mouth.

"God knows I want to fuck you right where you stand," he said in a whisper. "But you deserve better than this. I could make you come right now, under the moonlight, against this damn door – and I would hate myself for it."

With one final kiss, he stepped away from me, his chest heaving as he breathed.

Admittedly, I was desperate to see his home, his bed – to see where a genius laid his weary head every night. To lay beside him, be in his arms. He was right. It would be so worth it to wait.

And yet my body ached and throbbed right here, right now, contorting my face with the agony of it. An insecurity, borne of my past, rose slowly inside me like an ugly carp. The bullying, the ever-present disdain between me and my parents, all combined to resurface my weakness. What if he was merely putting me off? What if he was only biding his time, thinking of some way to let me down gently?

CHAPTER TEN

Wesley

The morning presented me with an unwelcome break in my routine, and I so loathed breaking routine. Especially when I had other things on my mind; namely one luscious, wanting, Jennifer Hurst.

As I made my way to the postnatal unit, I could still smell Jen's heat on my skin. Forcing away my desire was an uncomfortable task, but I was fast becoming besotted with her, and I couldn't let that show while I was working. She had disrupted my banal life in the most delicious way, and I owed her so much already. I needed to bed her soon or I would go utterly insane with my lust for her, but it had to be right.

Making it right for Jen was my only purpose, my only personal need, right now – and I was going to make it happen this evening.

Bitter regret made me wince as I strode into the postnatal unit, glancing up at the board to find my patient – Alfie Jones, a newborn. Now that I understood Jen's past, and had seen the criticisms she faced and the scathing looks of her own parents – who should have been bursting with pride to have a high-achieving, intelligent daughter like Jen – I felt sick to my stomach.

She'd already spent a lifetime trying to exchange her achievements for love and respect from her parents. What had I done, except prove I was just as bad as them – that I had expectations of personal sacrifice in exchange for her career progression?

I was wrong, for god's sake, and cruel. I didn't want to be cruel, and I certainly didn't like being wrong. Frankly, I wasn't used to it. Surgeons at the height of their game never were. Hartcliffe and Griffin were fine examples – both lucky in love and with careers – almost – as enviable as mine. But prove them wrong about something and you'd witness a meltdown of epic proportions. You'd need your running shoes.

And despite my own hubris, I supposed I was no better. We were egotists because life had given us blessings, allowing us to practice medicine, and it was all too easy to forget it. Our patients deserved better. Our interns deserved better.

I was going to make it up to Jen tonight, the

minute she walked through my door.

I cleared my throat and called through the blue curtain surrounding the bedchamber.

"Stephanie Jones?"

"Come in," she said.

I gently opened the curtain and stepped inside, finding an exhausted new mother sat up in bed, nursing Alfie to her breast. Immediately I could see the problem; at a few days old, Alfie's head should have formed a typical shape for a newborn, and I could see at a glance that it was misshapen. Still, I smiled and picked up the clipboard of notes at the foot of her bed.

"Stephanie, I'm Dr Brookes from the plastics department – I specialise in craniofacial surgery in children and babies. Did the paediatrician explain why I'd be visiting?"

"Yes," she said, looking pale and weary, no doubt existing on very little sleep. "His fontanelle was fused almost completely shut. He said there should be two fingers' width, but there was barely one."

"That's right," I said, gingerly making my way around her bed. As Alfie suckled contentedly, I took out a roll of measuring tape from my top pocket. "Do you mind if I take a look myself?"

"Of course not – can he keep feeding?"

"I wouldn't think of disturbing him," I said,

smiling. As I worked around Alfie and took my measurements, I held two fingers gently over his fontanelle and pressed. Then I felt around his soft cranium with my fingers, feeling the abnormalities.

I stood up, sighing. "According to the notes, his scans and examinations indicated no neurological abnormalities?"

"That's what they told me."

"And he's not had any seizures, no behaviours that concerned you?"

"I would have said if he had," she said, pressing her lips together in a hard line.

I could tell I was irritating her, but the questions had to be asked – several times, if necessary. It could be a real struggle to piece together a patient scenario when multiple disciplines were involved, passing information over patient notes or hasty phone calls. It was a big reason why I so loathed leaving my own department.

"Alfie's skull does appear to have fused early, but fortunately there don't seem to be any neurological symptoms – that is, he's showing no other signs of abnormality in the brain itself. With that in mind, our only risk is that Alfie's brain will be restricted as it grows, because there isn't enough space for expansion."

I explained that at around two or three

months of age, Alfie would need to undergo a minimally invasive procedure to open the fused section of his skull. After that, he could receive helmeting therapy to reshape his skull and allow for his brain to expand as it should when he grows.

"We'll continually monitor him to ensure the therapy is meeting our expectations. Do you need me to go over any of that again before I leave?"

Stephanie blinked and I realised she'd barely had a chance to digest my words before I was jetting off again. Of course she'd have questions – but I didn't have time for them, not now. I needed to get to clinic before I began the day's surgeries, and I was already losing time to get back on track.

I hadn't even had my morning cup of surgeon's tea.

"We can go over any questions you think of in clinic. I'll see you both in about two weeks' time with a fresh set of scans," I said, making to leave the cubicle.

"Wait, wait – is that it?" Stephanie looked dismayed as much as pissed off. She adjusted Alfie in the nook of her arm.

I cleared my throat, wringing my hands. "I can answer all your questions in our appointment. So unless there's anything urgent, I'm afraid I'm on an incredibly tight schedule –"

"Jesus," said Stephanie. "You don't waste a

lot of time on bedside manner, do you?"

I frowned a little, feeling confused. I'd been courteous as she nursed Alfie, I'd been minimally disruptive, I've given her all the facts...what else was there? I gave a brief apology and left, shaking my head. When I got back to my ward, I made an audible sound of joy and relief to see my tea waiting for me, along with the day's schedule.

Blessed routine, restored.

Janine was hovering, watching me as I took a grateful swig and acquainted myself with the day's activities.

Jen would be on the post-surgical ward doing her rounds right about now. I pictured her in her usual get-up of tight black pants and a buttoned white blouse, maybe with pinstripes. Her bust threatening to pop every one of those buttons off. Her silken blonde hair snaking over one shoulder, coiling around the neck I so enjoyed to kiss.

"What are you thinking about?" asked Janine. Her voice sounded strained, different, with an awkward upwards inflection that I didn't usually hear. It was enough to make me glance up from my schedule.

"Mm?"

"You've got a funny look on your face, like you're thinking about something silly. You're getting those cute blemishes you get when you're flustered," she said, reaching out and tapping me on the chin.

I shook my head, wondering what the hell had gotten into her. "Cute blemishes?" I asked aloud, as if she'd just given me the name of some foreign food.

Janine laughed, which in itself was unusual – I'd always known her to be fairly sombre.

"Actually, I did have a question," I said, desperate to get away from whatever weirdness was going on between us at this present time. "A patient of mine just now accused me of having a poor bedside manner."

"You? Never," said Janine, with a grin that did make me blush. Ah.

"And there was me thinking I'd improved over the years," I said, sighing. I took another long swig of my tea, conscious of time running out.

"You have," said Janine, rounding the nurses' station.

I noticed, then, that she was wearing a different uniform to her usual one. Janine usually wore the scrub suit in a dark navy blue – had done for years, in fact – but today she wore a tight-fitting pale blue tunic with sheer black tights. Janine was a woman in her prime, barely 30; she looked good. If she was trying to impress somebody, I was glad for her – I'd never known her talk of having a partner. Then again, I couldn't recall ever asking.

"You can't expect the patients to understand you like we do. Like *I* do," said Janine, approaching me slowly, playing with her fingers. I picked up on an anxiety, judging by her body language. That would have been an impossibility a few years ago, when I wouldn't have understood her behaviour at all. Reading social signals was a skill I'd needed to learn, which others took for granted.

"I should be grateful for you. You've the patience of a saint, Janine," I said, finishing my mug of tea and dangling it by the handle over the crook of my two fingers. "Listen, if you're about to spring some unexpected leave on me – "

"Leave? No, no. I – actually, I wondered if you could spare five minutes before clinic starts, Wes. I...there's something I need to talk to you about. Urgently," said Janine. I noticed her pale mocha skin flushing slightly red, and her fingers worked a strand of her hair, looping it around and around.

I groaned, glancing up at the analogue clock. She was right – there was a little time left.

"All right, my office, now – but we'll have to be quick. Can you be quick?" I asked.

"I think I can," she said, smiling in a knowing way that made me uncomfortable.

I led the way to my office, a knot of anxiety building under my ribs. I only wanted to begin my day – a routine, problem-free day, with any luck – and skip to the evening, when I could have Jen in my arms again.

No sooner had I closed the door did I find myself face to face with Janine, and barely an inch of space between us. She was youthful, pretty in a dark way with her inky black hair and make-up in shades of black and plum red. I could recognise her beauty; no doubt she was alluring to someone else. Just not to me.

"Janine, I – "

"Don't say anything," said Janine. "I've seen the way she looks at you...you know who I mean. It's been driving me crazy. I couldn't go another day without – "

I frowned, unable to comprehend what she could be getting at – and then she showed me. As she trust herself up on her tip-toes, Janine threw her arms around my neck and pressed her lips to mine. She was heated, passionate, her fingers clawing my hair as if she'd waited a long time, and was savouring this first opportunity to do it.

Instinctively I pushed back, taking Janine by the shoulders and furiously wiping at my mouth. Her plum red lipstick smeared the back of my hand like blood.

"Oh god, I'm so sorry. I'm *so* sorry, Dr Brookes."

"Janine, we – you – I can't – "

"It's okay, it's okay. You're still not ready." She was visibly shaking, her hands frantically smoothing down the front of her tunic. "I've been patient until now. I can wait a little longer. But god, Wes – I couldn't go another day without telling you how I feel."

I furiously wiped at the smear of lipstick on the back of my hand, anger twisting my face into an expression that made Janine shrink back toward my desk.

"This isn't acceptable, Janine. Not for me."

Her eyes widened with hurt. "But – you – but you knew, didn't you?"

"I had no idea."

She flinched as if I'd struck her. A heat rash clustered at her chest and made a patchwork up her neck. Budding tears glinted, catching the light. Her breaths came in shaking, uneven rasps.

"But I...I do everything you ask of me, Wes. Every morning I bring your tea, and print out your schedule. I run errands for you," she said, shaking her head in disbelief. "You had to know. I've been...fuck, Wes, I've been *dedicated* to you. I've done crap for you that's well below my pay-grade!"

"You are a wonderful charge nurse, and you know this department like the back of your hand. You are organised, efficient. Your command in the OR is famous across this hospital – nobody dares cross you," I said, trying to smooth things over. I did appreciate Janine. Just not like that.

Janine stepped forward, her expression

confused, questioning. I held her back by the shoulders, solemnly shaking my head. Her disappointment reappeared, her expression crestfallen.

"I think the world of you, Janine – professionally. That's all it is," I said.

I knew that this was not the most diplomatic or charming way to defuse what had turned out to be a monstrous misunderstanding, but the facts were the facts. I hadn't thought for a single moment that she could've planned to spring this on me now – not ever, in fact.

A deep frown contorted into a look of bitterness. "You let me do all these little extras for you because you think it's a...a what? A quirk of mine? That I enjoy being your personal assistant on top of *all* my other responsibilities?"

"I'm sorry, Janine. I would never intentionally disrespect you. But you have gotten the wrong idea," I said firmly.

Tears sprang from her eyes, which she furiously wiped away. She looked down, her eyelashes dark and wet. "You tell me all the time that you couldn't live without me."

Regret stung my core, then, to hear her say that. I'd been leading her on without even knowing it. I *should* have known.

"This department would fall to chaos without you. I wanted to make sure you understood my appreciation of you, so that you wouldn't want to leave," I said.

"Is that a fancy way of saying I was being used? That you were buttering me up so I kept making mugs of tea for you, and giving you heads ups, and coaching you on how to talk to people like a damn human being?" Janine's initial upset was now turning to fury. Her fists were balled at her sides as she let me have it.

"When are you going to *stop* using people, Wes? I knew you saw most people as – I don't know – tools, or useful parts, or something. But not me. I thought I was special to *you*."

"You are, Janine. You're my team mate, my –
"

"Just stop," she said, another stray tear escaping her deep onyx eyes. "I realise I've made an idiot of myself. It's my fault. I read into things, saw things that weren't there..."

Finally, I thought – she was understanding. Janine folded her arms across her chest, pacing back and forth before me.

"For a while I thought maybe you just didn't have it in you to – to love. Not after what Rebecca did to you. I thought maybe you were married to your work after that, and as long as I got to be by your side every day, that was good enough. We worked. You got colder, more set in your ways. I figured – hey, he's obviously still hung up on

Rebecca. I'll wait. Then *she* came, and I finally saw another side of you."

I cleared my throat, glancing anxiously at the time.

"Yeah, I know. We're on a schedule," Janine bit out, before returning to her point. "I thought she was just another girl with a crush. We get enough of those in this hospital. But then I started to see how you looked at *her*, too."

"It's not at all what you think, Janine. I have the utmost respect for Jennifer – "

"See. You knew exactly who I was talking about."

She'd got me, there – and it absolutely was what she thought. I'd been struck by Jen the moment she stumbled into the ward, late as she would always be, infuriating me from the second I set my eyes on her. Jen had looked up at me with an admiration and slight fear in her eyes that set my insides on fire, and my feelings had been growing ever since.

But Janine saw how I favoured her, and followed her every movement, and now I couldn't deny it any longer. I decided I would avoid it all together. We had to move on with our day.

"I'd appreciate it if we could keep this between ourselves, Janine. I'm sure you agree," I said curtly. I cleared my throat, looking anywhere but at her.

"It's way too late for that," she said, sighing. "There's a rumour going around that you're engaged. At first I couldn't believe what I was hearing – if Wes had someone special in his life, I'd be the first to know, right? Then I heard that you were supposedly engaged to *Jennifer*."

I wiped my face with my hand, wishing I could give my head a whack against the cold white wall.

"Well? Is it true?"

Jen had appreciated my well-intentioned parents immensely, but in that moment I could have killed them – presuming, of course, that they'd been the ones to spread the word. It could just as easily have been Jen's parents who'd passed the news on to their wider circle, having heard through the grapevine themselves, and they'd have more inclination to add a little malice to it.

I sighed, pinching the bridge of my nose. What had happened to my quiet, mundane existence? The extraordinary for me had become the hum-drum after a couple of decades in surgery, and I had been happy with that. Now I felt as though I was being evicted from my life. I could only blame myself.

"This has all gotten out of hand," I said, exasperated.

"You can't at least answer me? Wow. I thought more of you than this," said Janine, walking around me to the door. She kept her distance as if an invisible bubble prevented her from stepping within two feet of me. As she dipped the handle, she paused, glancing back at me. "Your bedside manner really does suck, by the way."

I folded my arms and watched Janine leave the room.

Now that I knew the news had been leaked to our department, it dawned on me that Jen would be drawn into the gossip, subjected to all the cruel remarks of our peers. I didn't give a damn what anybody who was entertained by gossip had to say, but that didn't mean Jen could brush them off so easily. She was young, still a fresh face in the game. If she was branded a teacher's pet, the label could follow her. Our peers would question every milestone and achievement in her career, asking if it was talent or favouritism that got her there.

A user. Janine had branded me a user who failed to consider his impact on others.

And apparently, she was right.

CHAPTER ELEVEN

Jennifer

Connie and I had just finished readying the patient and clearing the site when Wes entered the OR, gowned up and holding his gloved hands aloft.

I watched him, knowing I had felt his athletic, tight form with my hands, and had run kisses over that skin. The knowledge sent a shudder of desire through me. I hoped his emerald green eyes would look to me over his mask, but they looked only at the patient's exposed brow and cheek bone, the skin and flesh pulled away. My heart twisted like a knot pulled tight, and a sickening sensation came over me. Was he really avoiding my gaze?

I looked over twelve-year-old Jayden's sedated form. An emergency admission due to a car wreck, Jayden had been slotted to the front of the list, interrupting the day's schedule. I wondered if that was why Wes appeared so agitated – shifting his schedule around was a good way to piss Wes off, even if he did love the odd spontaneous surgery, with a new puzzle to solve.

I certainly did. Now that I'd really got to grips with re-constructive surgery, I knew that it was my true calling. I had him. Wes' beautiful hands worked the metal plate that he would be fitting against the boy's cheekbone.

"I need a 1a, 1b, and 2a," he said in a gruff voice. "Suction."

Janine applied the suction while while Dr Bingham excused herself, with her own surgery due to begin in the next OR – Jayden's school friend, who came off worse in the car wreck with a leg crushed, the bones splintered in several places. As Connie left, she caught my eye deliberately. She glanced at Wes and back at me, winking, with a twinkle in her deep eyes. I frowned, and she returned a mischievous smile.

"What?" I mouthed silently.

"Congratulations," she mouthed back, grinning, before slipping out of the OR.

Panicked, I glanced up at Wes and could have kicked him when he wouldn't look back at me. How? How could Dr Bingham know anything about us – let alone enough to say *congratulations*?

Then it dawned on me with a sickening wave of nausea. Shit. It had to be my parents – it just had to be. Maybe his, but I got the feeling they would let Wes take the lead and would respect his privacy until he was ready to share the news on a wider scale – a level of consideration that my parents would never give. In any case, Dr Bingham wasn't even the first person to wink at me that day. She was the third.

People knew about our "engagement", and things were going to become very complicated indeed. Never mind, I thought – we could hash out a plan tonight and figure out a way to weasel our way out of this before anybody started popping champagne. After I'd finished my own business with him, of course.

That is, if I ever caught up with him.

Wes escaped me even after surgery, dumping his gown and gloves and leaving the OR before I'd even had a chance to wash my hands. Now I was really freaking out, knowing I would need to corner him soon to calm my nerves and get some reassurance. I didn't know what we were, or what we were doing – but I knew I had to be near him, with him, or else I'd go mad.

We'd already gotten so close to being together. Last night I'd even dreamed of him inside me, filling me – and I'd been throbbing with the absence of him all morning.

I needed the real thing or else I felt like I'd go insane.

Janine appeared before me, with her usual expression of chewing a wasp. I noticed her eyes looked a little red today, her eyelids swollen, and her make-up was a little smudged – particularly at the corners of her mouth.

"I know you think you've got him, but you really haven't," she said, folding her arms and looking down at me like I was some sort of cockroach.

"Excuse me?" I asked.

"I've heard the rumours. Everybody has. But I just wanted to do you a favour, Jen – as someone who really knows Wes – and tell you that when it comes to him, you don't have the first clue," said Janine.

"You've lost me already," I said, smiling grimly. Whatever it was, I didn't care to hear it. Wes Brookes was not her concern, and I didn't care how many desperate mugs of tea she made for him.

"Have you ever seen a photograph of Rebecca?" she asked, making me stop abruptly mid-scrub. I glanced at her, watching her mouth curl up at the corner in a cruel smirk. "Wow. You don't even know about her, do you?"

"I don't care to discuss this with you," I said, turning the tap on full blast to rinse.

"You'll want to know all about her when you see her photo," said Janine, shaking her head as if she felt sorry for me. "We all knew her, all met her. Everybody in the department knew about about Wes' fiancé. He was obsessed with her; he'd do anything for her. Wes was beyond in love with Rebecca – even after she destroyed him."

My heart beat rapidly and a wicked jealousy clawed away at me, making me stagger back with my wet hands still dripping. He'd never mentioned an ex-fiancé, and now that I learned of her, I already despised her.

"It was me who was there for him every morning, every surgery, holding him up, keeping him going. He was a broken man, and it was me who picked up the pieces," said Janine.

I scoffed at that, unwilling to get her the satisfaction of knowing how devastated I felt.

"I'm sure you just hated doing that," I said. "Given you've been pining for him for god knows how long. Tell me – if you're so close to him, why don't you let him know that you're borderline obsessed with him?"

"He knows how I feel," she said flatly.

I winced. He hadn't told me that, either. Now I looked at Janine's imperfect make-up, especially the smudged lipstick, and wondered if she'd told him today – and just how she'd told him. The thought of her lips on his made me feel sick with envy, a territorial rage filling me. What if that explained his icy mood? Had she made him realise just what she could offer him, and he'd gone off me all together?

I had to wonder just how many women Wes had in his life. Was he ever planning on filling me in, or was I never supposed to find out? Suddenly I realised that despite our obvious attraction to one another, I barely knew Wes at all.

"If he knows then he doesn't want you, or else we wouldn't even be having this conversation," I said, wiping my wet hands on a blue paper towel. I dumped it in the bin.

"He'll come around," said Janine, making me want to grab a handful of her hair and rip it out. I balled my firsts at my side, breathing slowly, talking myself out of it. "He'll see sense eventually."

"That's pathetic," I said, shaking my head with a catty smile on my face. But it hurt, knowing he was being pursued – and not knowing whether he might cave in to the pressure. Not knowing if he already had.

"Not as pathetic as being a stand-in for the ex who broke his heart. You're a dead-ringer for her. How does it feel to know you're nothing but a cheap replacement?"

"Go get fucked, Janine," I spat out, storming past her and out into the hallway, where I practically had to gasp for air. I hurried to the staff bathrooms and managed to stave off my tears until I got to the stall at the very end, where I sobbed into a handful of tissues.

♥

I waited for him, quite pathetically, by his office. After he'd given the handover for the next shift, he'd disappeared, leaving me feeling dejected and pining after him. Still, his eyes hadn't met mine – not once. It was killing me to see him, wanting to touch him, and having no opportunity to.

Maybe, even, no right to.

As I paced, bowing my head and blowing out long streams of exhaled breath, a hand took me by the elbow. I span and came face to face with Wes, looking down at me with a grim expression. He wore tailored black trousers and a grey shirt with pinstripes, no tie.

"It's you," I said, breathlessly, reaching to take his hand – and finding he kept his grip at my elbow. "Wes?"

"Not here," he said, lowering his hand to take mine. He held it stiffly, practically dragging me out of the ward and out to the lifts. He wouldn't speak or look at me, even as we waited for the elevator car, nor the whole way up. As we reached street level, Wes' grip on my hand was fierce.

"What the heck are you doing? You're

hurting me!"

He let go of my hand as we approached a sleek black Mercedes. He opened the passenger door with one stiff jerk and waited for me to get inside. Tears pricked my eyes, but I got in, bracing myself for whatever hideous news he was saving for me.

He slammed the car door and entered the driver's side, pulling off and taking us out into the heavy London traffic. We shared an icy silence. Once we made some headway, I stole a glance at him and found myself wanting to sob. His face was ice cold, devoid of any emotion at all. His eyes were flat, appearing colourless and without dimension now that the life had gone out of them.

My pain turned to anger very swiftly.

"I know what you're going to tell me," I said, my chest heaving as I held back my tears. "She got to you, didn't she?"

A frown rippled his brow as he concentrated on the road, stopping at a set of red traffic lights. "Who?" he asked.

"You know who," I said. "If you want her, then you could spare me this horrible experience. You could have told me in the break room."

"I don't want her," he said brusquely.

"She thinks she's going to wear you down," I said, my voice weak and rasping. "That's what she said."

"Did she, now."

That comment made me look at him questioningly. I realised things weren't as Janine described – not to Wes, anyway – but my jealousy was tormenting me too fiercely for me to think rationally now. I squirmed in my seat, feeling as if something was gnawing away at my insides.

"I know she kissed you," I said, failing to hide the hurt in my voice.

Wes pressed his lips firmly together, hiding the masculine outline of his finely shaped mouth. "I didn't kiss her," he said.

A silence fell between us. For the rest of the car ride I stared out of my passenger window, watching St Paul's Cathedral go by and the heaving crowds of financiers and bank managers flooding out of their offices. It was icy, painful; so in contrast with every meeting I'd had with Wes before, where he'd filled me with warmth and desire.

He parked up in an underground car park and took my hand again, taking me into a foyer with gleaming marble floors and ceilings, and a colossal feature chandelier with long glowing glass cylinders. I realised by now that we were at least going to his apartment, but it did nothing to soothe the nausea in my stomach.

When we finally made it inside his corner penthouse apartment, I was taken aback

THE INTERN AND THE PLASTIC SURGEON

momentarily by the tasteful, homely interior. With its cream carpets and classic stained Art Deco wall sconces, it spoke of class and sophistication. I followed Wes through a traditional kitchen into a large living room with an enormous, wide corner window overlooking the Thames.

Wes indicated for me to sit on the sectional sofa. He took two glasses from a small bar on the wall beside the window and poured us both a glass of white, handing mine to me with a rigidity that made me want to cry. Wes remained standing and only leaned on a 30s style armchair in deep burgundy, his back to the beautiful glittering vista of London.

I gulped half the wine down, wincing as it burned my throat.

Finally, Wes spoke to me properly.

"I had so many plans for tonight, Jennifer. So many ideas. I wanted to show you my feelings for you in a way that was respectful, with the dignity that you deserved. I wish – I wish I'd thrown all that to hell and made love to you at the first opportunity," said Wesley, pacing in front of the glittering skyline.

A lump sat in my throat. Frankly, I'd wanted him to show me in every possible *undignified* way. I swallowed hard as I gulped down the rest of my wine in one go and set the glass down on the coffee table between us.

"You still can," I said.

To hell with it, I thought – Wes might be content being secretive, but I wasn't, not anymore. I wasn't holding back.

Wes closed his eyes briefly.

"Something was made clear to me today. Something I need to work on." Wes bowed his head, shaking it gently as he paced.

He finished his wine and set the glass down opposite mine. "I have a... A slight difficulty that I've been working on for a few years, now. I'm not so good with people; reading them, treating them the right way – it's a work in progress. I thought I was doing well, but I...apparently my involvement with you is clear evidence that I've made no progress at all."

"What the hell are you talking about?" I asked. "There's nothing wrong with you. You're just reserved, that's all. People get that. You're a doctor, not a party host."

He smiled, then, making eye contact with me. My heart leapt, realising there could be the slightest sliver of hope for us yet.

Then doubt clouded his face, and his frown returned.

"I don't think I'm any good for you, Jen. I can't be what you deserve, and you deserve the best. I've – I've used you. I've done the unthinkable. Now people are finding out, and I find myself feeling...ashamed. I'm afraid that if I go any further with you, it'll be another case of me selfishly taking what I want when I haven't even considered how this could impact you and your career."

"Bullshit," I said, making him flinch. He looked at me, astonished.

"Jen?"

"You heard me. What – do you think I'm some little kid? I'm a grown woman, Wes. I told you I wanted you."

"You agreed to a false relationship because I told you it'd further your career."

"And I knew exactly what I was getting into," I said. "What's offensive is that you think you know what's best for me, Wes."

He shook his head. "It's my role to guide you. I'm supposed to protect you and your interests, for Christ's sake – and look at what I've made of that task. I've twisted it into something that suits me, suits my needs – it's all I ever do!"

Wes' voice was raised, pained, and I knew he meant it. But I was going to stand firm.

"If that was true then you'd be thinking with your cock right now, and you aren't."

Though god, I wished he would.

"Can't you see I'm not any good for you?" he asked.

"You're my mentor – not my father. I don't need you to tell me what to do or how to run my love-life."

"I'm sorry, Jennifer. It's over for us. When we get back to the department tomorrow, we'll have to muster up the courage to continue as if this never happened. We'll dispel the rumours and tell our respective families that we're no longer a couple," said Wes, clawing his hands through his hair.

They'd gotten to him. They'd all gotten into his head. Janine, and both of my parents.

"All right, Wes. I'll believe it's over if you can convince me," I said, shrugging off my jacket and laying it over the back of the couch.

"How can I convince you?" he asked hopelessly. His eyes darkened as I began to unbutton my blouse, my gaze focused on him.

"Jennifer, don't do that," he said.

I let my eyes wander over his fine form, focusing on the delicious body that awaited me under his clothes. If he could resist me now, then I knew it was over for us – but if he couldn't, then I would show him just how decisive I could be. I'd make him forget all about everyone else.

I slowly peeled off my blouse and tossed it aside, before popping the button on my slacks and letting them drop to my feet. I stepped out of my shoes and made my slow way toward him , letting his eyes wander hazily over my lacy blue thong and plunge bra - ones I'd chosen especially for him.

"You think performing a strip-tease for me will change my mind?" his voice was strained, choked, and I already knew I was winning.

"I think a demonstration will assuage your doubts," I said, taking him by the hand and pushing him by his shoulder down into the burgundy armchair.

As he gazed up at me with desire in his eyes, I popped the clasp of my bra and let it drop to the floor. My breasts fell heavy and aching, out on display, my nipples already hardened to tender buds. I soothed the aching by cupping them, massaging them, before I gave my nipples a pinch. I kept eye contact with Wes the whole time, letting my lust for him build and spur me on. The bulge in his pants had swiftly grown to the obscene, clearly outlining a large, throbbing cock.

"You see what you do to me?" I asked him softly, as I climbed over his lap and straddled him.

His handsome face and head of luscious blonde hair was between my breasts, and I stroked him, coaxing him gently. His expression was pained as he attempted to resist me, closing his eyes and swallowing hard.

Within moments his eager mouth found my

left nipple, and against his own restraint, his lips closed around it. His cheeks hollowed as he sucked on it, his tongue rounding and nudging it until I moaned. Soon his hands were cupping my breasts, his fingers rolling and pulling my free nipple, while he sucked the other with a new desperation.

I panted as I unbuckled his trousers, aching to free the thick column that strained his pants. Reaching in to pull down his briefs, his swollen cock and laden ball sack fell heavily into my hands. His cock was velvety smooth with thick veins snaking its wide shaft, and the crest of its beautiful bulbous head was swollen and slightly purple in shade. The girth and length of him made my throbbing cleft cream with desire, my vaginal walls throbbing and aching to be filled with the glorious cock I held in both hands.

As my hands held him and gently began to caress, Wesley grunted, releasing a small, glistening spurt of pre-cum. I thumbed it, massaging it into the crown that I so desperately wanted to suck, to fuck, to feel nudging against the neck of my womb.

He released my nipple and muttered faint protests that I silenced with my deep kiss. I focused on his tongue, first, before licking his top lip and tracing the line of his scar. My clitoris pulsed with vigour as my tongue felt along the ridge of it, wanting his imperfect mouth to clamp around it almost as much as I wanted his cock deep inside me.

"Jennifer," he gasped against my lips.

"I don't know which part of you I want inside me first," I said breathlessly, clinging on with fistfuls of his hair. "I've wanted you since the moment I met you, Wesley."

"And god, I've wanted you," said Wes, his hands roaming my hips, my waist, before gripping hold of my bare buttocks.

Suddenly he lifted me, taking me to the sectional couch.

I writhed as he laid me down. Wes was still fully-clothed but for his freed cock, which stood upright as he moved me. I squirmed against the couch cushions, my sex pulsing, longing for him. He drew away my thong and threw it aside. I squealed as his hand cupped my entire vulva and massaged it, my juices soon glistening on his palm. He gently thumbed my clitoris, making me groan and clutch the cushions, lifting my hips and arching my back in pure pleasure.

I looked at him through my eyelashes, seeing him almost fully clothed and yet his arousal so obvious and bare under the dim lights, the head of his cock glistening. I thought my heart might stop at the sight of him above me, taking control of me. He slipped one finger in and probed me gently at first, then began a rhythm as he slid in a second.

"You're so hungry for me, Jennifer. Your slit

is so tight around my fingers." He thumbed my clitoris as he probed.

My hands roamed my body as I squirmed under his expert touch, my fingers rounding my nipples to pinch and ease the aching of them. Wesley took over, first with one hand, and then the other as he slid it gently from my wanting passage. He pinched and rolled my nipples, before his hands left me completely. I opened my eyes, groaning at the loss of him – but what I saw sent a new ripple of lust through me.

He unbuttoned his shirt and tossed it aside, before stepping out of his trousers, socks, and shoes. The breath stopped in my throat as I laid bare before him, looking up at his smooth, muscular body, with his tousled hair and emerald eyes looking down at me in my most vulnerable form. My memory took me back, instantly, to the first moment I saw him – when I was beneath him, looking up at those eyes, quivering under his gaze.

Now his cock was at full mast above me, thick and veined and wanting me.

Towering above me as he was, with his lean muscular build and locks of golden hair, he looked like a work of art – like the statue of David. He straddled the couch, the carved muscles flexing in his thighs and calves. He lifted me under the thighs and nestled his head down between my legs.

I mouthed obscenities as his tongue first probed my vagina, stroking at its pulsing walls, before he drew it back out and licked in slow circular motions around my clitoris. I found myself moving and gyrating to his rhythm, climbing, climbing, until his lips closed around it completely and sucked. The ridge of his scar prodded and nudged, adding texture that made me grind and writhe for more. His tongue pushed my clit directly as he drew on it, making me cry out-loud.

My climbing reached its peak and I bucked hard, crying his name as I came. Euphoria flooded me, making me claw the couch cushions.

Still gasping, I was caught off-guard by the hot nudging of his cock at my entrance. He had shifted to an upright position, his mouth wet and his face flushed, his eyes narrowed on me.

"I badly need to fuck you, Jen," he said with a thick, strangled voice. "Are you – do you – "

He seemed desperate, impatient. Even in the fog of my come-down, I knew what he needed to know.

"I'm on the pill," I said, panting – grateful that I had kept taking it despite my pact to stay single. "You could fill me with your creamy, delicious seed and I would only want more of it. I need you, too."

Wes grunted and drew me up into his lap

LIZA COLLINS

in one sweep, filling my mouth with his wanting tongue as he kissed me, passionately, as if to devour me. A light sweat bathed our skin. Wes' skin had a velvety touch as I melted into his arms, pressing myself against his warm, naked form, wanting to drown in him.

I pressed him back against the sofa, eliciting a questioning look on his chiselled face. I held his firm shoulders as I straddled him, wet and throbbing and aching to receive. Wes smoothed the hair from my face and kissed me softly, breathlessly.

"What are you doing, my darling?"

"I need you like this," I said, letting the rounded crown of his cock nestle against my sex. I was ready for another orgasm, and I wanted to take it from him. I freed my hair from its elastic and let it tumble free about my face and shoulders. Wes sighed and ran his hands through it, sifting it through his fingers as he cupped the back of my head.

"You're an angel," he said.

I let the weight of my body push his head inside me, nudging him in just an inch. His cock head stretched me, moistening me, as I edged down further. I closed my eyes and drew in long, shallow breaths, before releasing them slowly. He was stuffing me to capacity, and yet my sex pulsed and released slick creamy fluid, easing his passage. Wes held me under my thighs and shifted me gently, shunting me further down his shaft. I splayed my legs either side of his carved Adonis belt, flattening at the base of him as we reached the hilt.

His delicious crown nudged a sweet, soft spot by the opening of my womb, making me groan before I'd even begun to move. I lifted myself with my forearms resting on his shoulders, letting my slickness ease our way. Wes caught me with one hand at my waist, and the other under my buttock, gyrating his hips expertly, rhythmically, to continue nudging that spot.

I arched my back, panting and moaning, my hands desperately clutching his hair. He angled himself just so that his pubic mound rubbed my aching clitoris, grinding and gyrating, until I reached an unbearable peak and shattered. I threw back my head and cried aloud as white spots danced behind my eyes, wave upon wave of a new orgasm crashing through me.

I melted into Wes' arms and fell helplessly into his kiss. Desire rose up in me again as he grunted, his eyes darkened like two black stones as his need took over him. He held me by the hips, shifting me back to give him the best angle to fuck me. I leaned forward and began thrusting, his face contorting as I took over and began to bounce, fucking him myself.

"God, *Jen*."

Wes' expression was pained as I pulsed up and down, his hands tightening on my hips with the desire to go full-pelt in the race to orgasm. I held him back, making him wince and groan helplessly under the rhythmic pounding of my slit. I maintained pace until his eyes opened, his head falling back on the back of the sofa, his neck strained.

"Fuck, fuck, *Jen* – "

At his strangled cries, I bent forward and thrust hard up and down, faster and faster, until Wes greedily slammed his cock back into me. Unable to hold back, Wes dug his fingers into my hips and I let go, allowing him to pound me to the finish line. He roared deliciously as his orgasm struck, giving him at first a pained expression, soon relinquishing to one of a soft, gasping vulnerability.

He rocked my body and stopped abruptly as he spurted his hot fluids into my passage, soothing me with his warm balm. His cock stiffened upright, hard as rock, as ropes of ejaculate shot from its head. The pulsing of him made me groan and sigh, wanting to build up to another orgasm. Wes' face softened, his breaths heavy and his hard chest heaving as he folded me into his arms, slowly coming back down to earth.

We slid into a laying position, me curled inside his arms, panting against his chest. His still-hard cock slid out of me, his warm juices spreading down my thigh. His lips found mine, pressing soft, exhausted kisses as I rested my head on his biceps.

His hand found my cheek, softly stroking, brushing me with the backs of his fingers. As I hovered gently on the edge of sleep, a thrill passed through me as I acknowledged that those hands had fixed thousands of faces, repaired and restored thousands of bones and soft tissues, and here they were mine to kiss and caress; mine to enjoy, to prod me and stroke me to orgasm.

"I love you, Jennifer," he said softly, making my heart heave with yearning.

His hand found my left nipple; found it erect and aching from the moment those words hit my ears. He rolled it and pinched it, making me squirm in his arms. I moistened for more.

"I love you too, Wes," I whispered, as his hand drifted down my tummy, stuffing two fingers inside my still-throbbing cleft. He massaged his semen into me, making me writhe –

Making me his.

CHAPTER
TWELVE

Wesley

Jennifer nuzzled against my biceps as I planted soft kisses on her cheek, her chin, and finally her lips. I stroked her hair and enjoyed the way the soft warm light pouring in from my large bedroom window bathed her in a honeyed glow. As she snuggled in closer to my body, still half asleep, she let out a soft giggle. I flexed my hard length against her smooth belly.

"He was awake before either of us was," I said, joining her laughter.

I planted soft kisses along her jaw and down her neck, coaxing her until I could feel her nipples tighten and harden against my chest. She rolled onto her back as I continued kissing, first down her chest and then around each breast, being slow and sensual as I led up to her prominent nipple. I hollowed my cheeks and drew on it, turning it around with my tongue, making Jen moan and clutch the pillow behind her head.

I drew my kisses back up her body before I devoured her mouth, lazily sliding my tongue across hers. As Jen began to grind as much as she moaned, I knew she was ripe for my cock. I took her missionary style, wasting no time. Judging by the angle of the sun, it had to be almost 7.00 a.m.

We'd need to be showered, fed, and in clinic by 8.30 a.m. – and we had the London traffic to contend with.

Jen's eyes hadn't even opened fully yet when she spread her legs and pulled me in toward her. Her hands sought my buttocks greedily, holding them as they tightened and flexed with my shifting movements. I nudged the sensitive, round head of my cock against her pulsing sex and drew in a slow, deep breath. Jen's eyes fluttered half open, watching me, begging me.

"Fuck me, Wes," she said sleepily. "Make me come."

I groaned as I heaved my cock in with one thrust, making her squeal faintly with sleepy pleasure. She lifted her legs so that her calves rested on my buttocks, allowing me easy passage as I began to pump back and forth inside her. Her beautiful face looked pained as she clutched my arse tightly, and I ground my hips in rhythm with hers, knowing I was nudging her sweet clitoris as I pumped.

I lifted my torso and caged her with my hands either side of her on the mattress. I watched her two plump breasts bounce with every thrust, her nipples erect with longing, and found myself pounding her harder and harder. I muttered sinful words as I fucked her, feeling her molten core moisten and give way to me, fitting hot and snug around my girth. As I plunged and felt the end of her, I moaned aloud, struggling to hold back any longer.

"*Wes!*" Jen cried, clutching my buttocks and forcing me against her in rough pulses. Her agonised expression gave way to euphoria and vulnerability as she let out repeated cries, before dissolving into a long sensual moan. Her vaginal walls pumped repeatedly around my cock, making me grit my teeth as I bared down against the urge to fuck fast and rough. I waited until her cries faded to go like a piston, climbing swiftly to my own hard, hot orgasm. She panted and cried as I reached my peak and stiffened, pumping hot spurts of my seed deep inside her. I groaned with every long shot, barely softening as I came down from my high.

Jen laced her fingers behind my neck and smiled at me in a way that made me melt.

"Good morning, handsome," she said with a

grin, her chest heaving, her skin bathed in a light sweat.

I held her tight to me and flipped us so she was on top of me, cupping her breasts and fondling them. Her hair tumbled about her shoulders; with her pale beauty and gleaming blue eyes, she looked like an English rose, a true princess.

I stiffened again just looking at her there above me, remembering how she'd straddled me the night before. I tweaked her nipples and pinched repeatedly, just gently, making her writhe and squirm. I could feel the wetness of my seed leaking onto me, making me rock-hard to know I'd marked her, made her mine again.

"We have just over an hour until clinic," I said, softly. "You'll have to wear scrubs, unless you want one of my shirts."

Jen smirked. "Sure, let's make it really obvious."

I shrugged. "People think we're engaged. What difference does it make?"

She looked up, considering it – and nodded appreciatively.

"True," she said. "Maybe I *should* wear one of your shirts and really piss Janine off."

I chuckled, squeezing her tits affectionately. I gently spanked her bare buttock. "Don't be tacky, darling – it's beneath you."

"Actually, you're beneath me," she said, bending to kiss me with her luscious lips.

I sat upright and hooked an arm under Jen's legs, carrying her to the shower. I kissed her long and deep, cradling her as I let the water run. As the steam formed, I stepped inside and planted her on her feet, pulling her into my arms. I turned her in my embrace so that her bum nestled against my burgeoning new erection.

Lathering up the soap in my hands, I ran them all over her, coating her in a soapy white foam that picked out the curvaceous line of her. Jen tilted her head back and moaned as the hot water soaked her hair, neck, and shoulders, which I massaged deeply as I washed her.

When my slick, soapy hands rounded on her breasts, Jen sighed and turned in my arms, pulling me into a deep, slow tongue kiss. She let the tip of hers flick my top lip, concentrating on the scar that I loathed and yet she seemed so obsessed with. It fast became an erogenous zone, knowing that it turned her on to feel it, keeping her moist and throbbing for me.

Jen washed my hair, massaging my scalp as I leaned my forehead against hers, wishing we could stay here all morning.

"We need to get out now, beautiful," I said, tipping my head back to let the water rinse my hair.

"What about if we were just a little late?" Jen asked in a sensual, pleading voice. Her hand circled the base of my cock and began softly pumping it, cupping my balls with her free hand. Instantly I surged with pleasure, groaning under her touch.

"We can't be late, darling," I said, gasping as she brought me closer with each stroke. "You know that."

"All right," she said, with a smirk. "We won't be."

Before I could protest and force my way out of the lustful fog that had fallen over me, Jen was on her knees. She pumped my cock as her full lips took the swollen head in her mouth, sucking and bobbing, drawing her tongue along the underside in a motion that drove me immediately to the cusp of coming. I strained and groaned, gritting my teeth as my hands found her wet hair. Despite my restraint, my hips began to grind and buck, and my hands pulling her, fraught with desire.

"God, fuck, *Jennifer* – "

I unloaded ropes of silken come into Jen's suckling mouth, lost in euphoria as her angelic face serenely took it all. She swallowed several times, gently pulling her lips away. Two latent shots of come hit her breasts as she looked up at me, the water washing them away.

"You owe me one at lunch," she said, holding my hands as she stepped to her feet. She shut the water off and stepped out, while I remained in a post-come headiness.

As we towelled off together, I found myself drawn to Jen's gorgeous figure and her luscious, perfectly round breasts. How could I leave her without another orgasm after she'd given me that?

"Ugh," I grunted, scooping her up in my arms. Jen let out another squeal, her towel dropping to the under-heated tile as I strode from the bathroom with her in my arms. I threw her down on the bed and lifted her thighs, nestling between her legs where I buried my face in soft, hot folds of her. One orgasm rolled into another as I tongued and suckled her with gusto, devouring her pretty little slit until I felt I'd rewarded her enough.

For now.

♥

As we finally neared Sacred Heart, I noticed Jen's bare ring finger as she rested her hand on her knee. She'd stopped wearing her false engagement ring after the evening with her parents, but its absence now felt wrong to me. Every day that Jen wasn't engaged to me now felt like an insult to her – as if she'd been good enough for pretending, but only girlfriend material in reality.

My rational mind reminded me that we'd only just admitted our love for one another – that it was far too soon to talk about engagements.

Another part of me wanted the world to know Jennifer was mine; to claim her and make it known with a statement for all to see.

Deep in thought, I almost missed that a silence had developed between us that Jen wasn't filling with chatter. I glanced at her, seeing a frown line between her eyebrows.

"What's the matter, darling?" I asked, wondering how she could possibly be wearing that face when we'd woken up the way we had.

I felt her face shift to me in my periphery, her expression pained and questioning.

"I wasn't going to say anything," she said, sighing. "But I need to know."

"Need to know what?"

She paused, moistening her lips with her tongue. "Who is Rebecca?"

I slammed on the brake, realising I was about to run through a red light. Someone on the oncoming side blared their horn. A tension headache rose up behind my eyes. How in hell had she learned about Rebecca?

"I don't know what you're referring to," I said, my throat feeling tight. The collar of my shirt seemed to be strangling me.

Jen sighed. "Wes, come on. Don't hold back from me."

Palpitations fluttered behind the walls of my

chest as I drummed the steering wheel, wishing the fucking light would change already.

"Wes."

"What is it? Look, there is no Rebecca to speak of."

Jen threw her head back against the head rest, making a disgruntled sound. "How can you say you *love* me if I'm not even allowed to know about your past?"

I felt myself shutting down, the walls rising up around me. I thought I was over Rebecca – for heaven's sake, I *was* over Rebecca. But I still couldn't talk about her because that involved Theo, my best friend since school, and the pain made me feel violent. Even saying her name out loud as I had was a push too far, making me want to put in my own driver-side window with my balled fist.

Jen took my silence and shook her head despondently.

"I can open up to you," said Jen.

I sighed. "Not now, Jennifer. We're nearly at work."

"I was in a long-term relationship with Graham, a pharmacist. My parents loved him – that should have been my first clue. He bullied me almost the entire time we dated.

"I was bullied the entire time I was in boarding school, too. I was a fat band kid with an acne problem – I have pictures. The trauma of the rejection I faced day-in, day-out, nearly ended me several times. My parents knew all about it and they were fucking useless," said Jen, letting it all out in one go.

"My only source of pride was my academic achievements. I thought if I could just give my parents what they really wanted, then I'd have what I craved the most – acceptance and approval."

She scoffed, chucking her head back. "Well, you know how that turned out."

"My beautiful, brilliant Jennifer," I said, letting my hand leave the wheel a moment to squeeze her knee. "I know how painful bullying can be, remember. I've been there too."

"I know," said Jen. "But it feels good to finally tell you."

I wasn't at all surprised to hear that Jen had been a brilliant, misunderstood child who blossomed into this astonishing woman in my passenger seat.

"Extraordinary people are rarely accepted in society," I said, turning into the Sacred Heart underground car park. "And you are the most exceptional person I've ever met."

As I parked, Jen's hand shot out and grabbed mine, closing around it. I sighed, my other hand on the door release button.

"Now I've shared with you, you share with

me," she said, eyeing me steadily. "Tell me about Rebecca."

"No," I said firmly.

My barriers were up, and there would be no way on god's green earth that I would be lowering them – certainly not when we were moments from starting clinic, and we were decidedly late already.

"Wesley, you have to tell me. Maybe not right now, but at some point, and soon. I need to know, okay? You can't just shut me out like this while claiming you love me!"

"I do love you," I told her, holding up her hand and kissing her knuckles. "I've been falling desperately in love with you since the moment you stumbled your way into my world."

Her shoulders softened, a smile teasing the corners of her mouth.

I sighed. "I will explain, Jen. I will. But not here, and not now."

That seemed to satisfy her, for now. She looped her bag over her shoulder, wearing yesterday's clothes that she would change into scrubs. As we walked toward the building, I took Jen's hand in mind and held it firm, showing her that I was hiding nothing. I was certainly not hiding her. She smiled triumphantly, squeezing my hand in return.

She felt so, so very right with her palm against mine.

As we approached the department, I glanced around us to check the coast was clear for some inappropriate workplace behaviour. When I was satisfied we were safe, I cupped her chin between my thumb and forefinger and pulled her in for a kiss.

"I'll see you in surgery, Dr Hurst." I whispered in her ear before planting a soft kiss on her lobe.

"I'll see you before then," said Jen, digging her lanyard out of her bag. "I'm bringing you your stupid tea from now on. If that bitch goes anywhere near the kettle, I won't be held responsible for my actions."

I chuckled, surprised at how delighted I was at Jen's possessiveness of me. I hadn't realised I would cherish that, of all things – knowing that she wanted to claim me, just as I wanted to claim her.

"Never again will a drop of Janine's tea touch my lips," I said, smirking. Poor Janine. She was a valued member of my team, but she could never be my beautiful, exceptional Jennifer.

Once again my eyes wandered to her bare ring finger, wondering how long I could stand to see it empty, with no symbol of my love – a feeling I never thought I'd experience again for as long as I lived.

Rebecca had been given that same gesture

of promise; a solitaire diamond on a solid gold band. She'd used it to destroy me; wore it while she defiled everything I thought we meant to one another.

And with my best friend, too.

CHAPTER THIRTEEN

Jennifer

As I closed up my locker and stepped out onto the ward in my blue scrubs, my heart gave palpitations. Wes Brookes. I was in love with my mentor, Wes Brookes – and I'd spent the night in his beautiful apartment.

As I checked the board for the day's surgical schedule, I thought only of Wes; of his bare beautiful body, the hard muscles of his arse flexing in my hands as he took me. Of the gorgeous naked form of him that nobody but me got to see. A ripple of pride and euphoria went through me, my mind delivering flashbacks of our insatiable lovemaking. My clit pulsed and my womb tightened just at the thought of having him again – maybe even tonight. Maybe lunchtime.

I ducked into the medicine room, the refrigerator humming behind me, and sent Wes a quick text – *bunk room, 2.30 break between patients, you and me*.

Despite my anger about Rebecca, and all the knowledge I *didn't* have about her, my lust for Wes superseded all that. I'd carp on about her again once I'd had my orgasm.

"Sounds good to me," said Wes' voice from somewhere behind me.

I span, seeing him standing there by the refrigerator, writing up his withdrawal of drugs on the chart. He smirked a little, never taking his eyes off the chart to look at me. He was dressed in full surgical scrubs for an early start, and my god, he looked so damn fine. His scrub shirt sleeve stopped just shy of the thickest part of his biceps, making my vaginal walls give a throb. His hair curled from beneath his surgical cap, and his large hands were bare, clean, working the pen over the surface of the paper.

How I wished for them to be working over me.

"I had no idea you were in here!"

Wes flipped the pages over and smiled wryly as he slotted the chart back in its holder on the wall beside the fridge.

"Slacker," he said, approaching me slowly.

He hooked a hand at my waist and pulled me

in, pressing me close against the dips and mounds of his muscular body. Instinctively I slipped a hand under his scrub top, feeling the ripples of his abdominal muscles. My free hand slid up his neck and around the back of his head, drawing him to me.

Wes kissed me softly at first, drawing me into his warm embrace, before his kisses became deep and passionate, making my knees shake.

"Where are you supposed to be right now?" he whispered against my lips as he pulled away.

"Post-op rounds," I said, nuzzling his nose. "Checking up on my little boy, Dylan, with the cleft palate."

Wes straightened, holding me by the shoulders. I searched his emerald eyes, wondering what he was thinking – wondering if every child with a cleft palate brought back bad memories of his own.

"You'll find he's recovering very nicely, because the surgeon who performed the repair from start to finish happens to be my wonderfully talented intern," said Wes, planting a single soft kiss on my lips. "That child reflects all the progress you've made."

"Under your leadership," I added, kissing his chin. "But I'll certainly take the credit."

"There's something else on your mind," said Wes, stroking my hair. "What is it?"

"You mean other than your horny-bitter charge nurse and your ex fiancé?" I asked, holding back the irritation I felt, once again. I couldn't afford to get in a state over this, even though it bothered me immensely – not here, anyway.

Wes closed his eyes slowly and opened them again, as if I'd said something really stupid. "Other than that."

I hugged him around the waist, pressing my face between the mounds of pectoral muscles. When I resurfaced, I traced the line of his beautiful scar with my fingertip.

"My patient made me think of you. His repair will barely show a scar once it's healed."

"Mine was rather more complicated," said Wes, in a matter-of-fact tone that didn't betray any emotion at all. "It took several stages of surgery. I had a rare case. Some of those surgeries couldn't be completed until I was ten years old. My face went through many changes, many of them ugly. Hence the name-calling."

I cupped my hand either side of his handsome face and wondered how he could have possibly been considered ugly, no matter what stage of repair his palate was in.

"Your scar is beautiful, and I would have loved you," I said softly.

He smiled. "And I would have loved you. Band outfit, acne, you name it."

Wes held me close and dipped me, kissing me so sensually that I felt it in my core. When he levered me up again, he walked away, still holding my hand until the very last moment when he was forced to let go.

"Until the bunk room, then," he said, smirking.

I took a moment to collect myself before leaving the room, feeling flushed and riled up. Maybe working so closely with the man I loved wasn't the best idea – not if I had a prayer of remaining professional.

Stepping into the hallway, my day got immediately worse as I bumped straight into Janine. Literally.

She stumbled aside, dropping her collection of papers. They fluttered all over the blue lino floor.

"Crap, I'm sorry," I said, stooping to help her pick them up. They were patient lab requests.

"I stacked them in order of importance for the tech," she said through gritted teeth as she plucked the sheets one by one from the floor. I handed my stack back to her and she snatched them, her nostrils flaring like a fire-breathing dragon.

"Asked him about Rebecca yet?"

I folded my arms, determined not to let her get to me this time. "We've set time aside. He's going to explain everything to me."

Janine snorted. "He's not going to say a word. He can't. He gets all choked up."

"He'll tell me," I said. "He loves me."

A bitterness flitted across her expression for a moment, before it was replaced with another wry smirk. "Seen a *photo* of her yet?"

"Shut up, Janine. Why don't you get laid, or something?"

Her laughter followed me as I stormed away, regretting my comment the moment I left. I knew all I was doing was feeding her by responding to her, giving her material to work with. What Wes and I had was real, and his ex wouldn't stand in our way any more than mine would. Certainly no spurned charge nurse was going to convince me otherwise.

My phone vibrated in my pocket. I sighed, ducking into the staff toilet on Pelican Wing to see what it was before I became tied up with my patient. Dylan's mother was eager to get him home, and if he had healed as expected over the last few days, he would be able to continue his recovery at home. I was especially looking forward to telling his mother that. Dylan himself was only a year old, but his mother's joy would give me a bounce in my step the rest of the day.

I answered without reading the name, and groaned inwardly as my mother's voice murmured in my ear.

"I wanted to tell you how ashamed I was when you left our dinner the other night," said my mother, her voice tight.

"Ashamed of your behaviour? You should be," I said in a clipped tone. "What do you want, mum? I'm working."

"I wanted to make sure you'd ended it with that groomer," she said.

I rolled my eyes, realising she'd fallen to new depths. "We're adults, mum. He's not my school teacher. There has been no grooming."

"He's a consultant and he crossed a line that one should *never* cross with a student," said my mother; I could almost feel the heat from her seething against my ear.

"Not a student, mum. Oh, and I should thank you for spreading the news of our engagement – apparently everybody knows."

"They should know! They should know what a disgrace he is. Your father and I raised you to do better than this. You've brought shame on your profession before you've even begun."

I scowled, running my hands through my ponytail. Clearly my mother wasn't very observant – staff got together left, right, and centre in Sacred Heart. "I can't deal with this right now, mum. I have a patient waiting."

Stuffing the phone in my pocket, I blinked away tears as I made my way to Dylan. A weight had gathered on my shoulders; a strain that threatened to buckle me. Wes had filled me with so much pleasure that morning that I felt I was being dealt a punishing reminder: that I didn't deserve this level of happiness. That it really was too good to be true.

I needed Wes. I needed his body, his expert tongue, his hands that took me away from all the pressures of life on a wave of ecstasy. How had I ever lived without that? Our date in the bunk room could not come fast enough.

As I entered Dylan's room, I found him sitting upright on the play mat, stacking blocks with his mother. He grinned a gap-toothed smile, so radiant and perfect, that it took my breath away. When his surgical site healed properly, he'd have barely a scratch to show for it.

I pressed my lips together, my tearful eyes meeting Dylan's mother's. She, similarly, was emotional at my obvious pleasure to see him doing so well.

As I wiped a stray tear and went to join them on the play mat, I knew there was more to it than simply a successful surgery. I was tearful because I'd been emotionally batted from pillar to post just on the walk down here. Seeing Dylan reminded me of what it was all for; why it was all worth it. I had to keep fighting against them – my parents, Janine, and anyone else. Maybe even Wes. Maybe Rebecca.

But I needed to know who I was dealing with first – and Wes was going to damn well fill me in.

♥

When I slipped into the bunk room, Wes was already there, waiting for me. He rose from his seated position on the lower bunk and stood, watching me, making my heart ache. I had so many plans for how I was going to broach the subject; how I was going to make him tell me all about Rebecca before he was ever allowed a hand on me.

But the moment I saw his strong, loving arms, I flew into them, holding him tight around his lean waist. The stress of the morning, with Janine and my parents and all the fear and doubt that flooded my mind as a result of them, all churned inside me like a storm only he could protect me from.

Wes held me, squeezing me tight as he felt me sob.

I told him in a shaking voice what had happened, and he drew me into him, soothing it all away with one kiss. My hands began to paw at him desperately, pulling up his scrub top and then tugging down his pants. Someone could walk in on us at any moment, but I didn't care. All I thought about was getting Wes between my thighs; to be pummelled greedily until I forgot everything, riding instead on wave after wave of euphoric orgasm.

Wes delivered, taking advantage for himself while he was at it, until we laid panting and sated in one another's arms.

Wes played idly with my nipple, rolling it between his thumb and forefinger, as we cooled down. Tucked against his chest, my stomach tightened in knots as I realised that I was going to ruin the beautiful moment by asking.

But I had to ask.

"Wes – will you tell me about Rebecca?"

His silence was his answer. His fingers paused their play on my nipple, his hand dropping to my hip.

"*Wes*? You said you would. I need to know, right now, or it's going to drive me mad."

He planted a placating kiss on my forehead, which only irritated me more.

"Not here," he said, sitting up.

I watched him incredulously as he pulled on his briefs and scrub pants, before shrugging on his scrub top. He'd be headed to the showers and to fetch a new pair of scrubs, just as I would, and then we'd be going our separate ways. I'd have to live with this anxiety until I saw him tonight – *if* I saw him tonight.

"When, then? Tonight? Will I see you tonight?"

Wes sighed, pulling down the hem of his scrub top. "I'm not sure about that. I've a call-out to Royal London this afternoon, and it could be a late one."

I frowned, sitting up. I pulled on my scrub top and searched for my underwear.

"And why am I not joining you?"

"Because I need you here, assisting Dr Bingham with the skin graft at three o'clock."

I cursed. These were all legitimate reasons why we should be apart, but they felt like lame excuses nonetheless.

"Fine," I muttered, aggressively tugging up my scrub trousers. "Fuck me then, I guess."

"Jen, my darling, come on. You must have known it would be this way, with our schedules – "

"Do *not* darling me," I said, glaring at him. "When you're ready to tell me about Rebecca, you call me. Until then, I don't want so much as a text message."

"*Jennifer* – "

"Just answer me one thing, then. Is this all still a big game of play-pretend for you? Are you just trying me out, as a replacement for the woman you *really* want?"

He looked hurt, then, his eyes closing as he swallowed hard. "No. Don't ever think that. This felt real to me from the moment you walked up to my parents' doorstep. I never needed to pretend with you."

A clenching sensation took over my heart. It had felt real to me from that moment, too. After my stunt with the engagement ring, my performance ended.

"If that's true, Wes, then you need to understand this. I need to know who she was, and why she has such a hold over you. I need to know if you're really as invested in me as I am in you. I *need* to know if I have competition."

"You have *no* competition, Jen!"

"Then prove it to me," I said, my hand holding the door handle. "Because I'm not sharing you."

I left him standing there, my heart and gut wrenching. A horrible dread came over me as I walked, knowing that if Wes couldn't open up to me, then we would never make it.

We would be over before we'd even begun.

CHAPTER FOURTEEN

Wesley

How – how was I ever going to tell Jen about Rebecca?

She was too persistent for me too put it off for ever, and she was right. I did owe her at least some insight into my world, or else we'd never bond on an intimate level. But I didn't operate like that, not ever – nobody knew me. My colleagues were my friends, and we kept our professional boundaries in place. We talked shop. We didn't talk about heartbreak.

As I buckled my trousers and dressed in my shirt and tie, I remembered my final conversation with Rebecca – raw, painful. Unforgettable.

You want to know why it happened? I'll tell you. It's because outside of a bedroom, you've got ice in your veins. Theo talks to me, makes time for me. You take me for granted!

A shiver ran up my spine as I shrugged on my grey woollen coat.

Some of what she'd said was true – I did take her for granted. But that was because we'd seemed like such a sure thing for so many years that I couldn't imagine it being any other way. When I became so deeply involved in my work that I began to neglect her, I'd never considered for a moment that she'd leave me – and certainly not the way she did.

I thought we'd weather all storms together, but Rebecca took the first route out with Theo. She fell at the first hurdle.

And if she could do that, well…she can't have ever really loved me.

I searched the hall for Jen, hoping I'd get a chance to hold her and kiss her before I left for the Royal London hospital.

I was needed to assist a tumour removal that would require several bone grafts, and I would be using my Brookes Bolt to form the proper attachments. It was a surgery estimated to last between six and eight hours, which meant I wouldn't have a chance to be with Jen. My chest tightened as I failed to spot her among the busy bays, knowing that she already felt I was shutting her out. What if a few hours was all it took for her to give up on me?

The first thing I would tell Jen about Rebecca would be that I'd spent years dedicated to her, and it still hadn't been enough to keep her.

I would tell her that her deceit had haunted me for years after, that it gave me a fear of abandonment and coloured the way I treated people. It created a lack of trust that I hadn't experienced since school, when friendships were difficult to make.

I could tell her that it's the real reason why I asked her to be my fake girlfriend in the first place.

I wanted to hide my obvious torment by pretending to have moved on...and then the most magical feelings had grown between me and Jen, and she began to heal those wounds.

That would be a start.

Jen would be patient with me – she was kind, caring. I knew I could make her understand the moment I found some real time to talk to her.

But for now, my duties to my patient came first.

As I left the tree-lined entrance to the hospital, my phone hummed in my pocket. It was Mr Griffin, whom I would be working with to excise this patient's tumour. I knew instantly that something had to have gone wrong.

"It's a no-go I'm afraid, Brookes. The

patient's running a fever and their white cell count was concerning. We're going to hold off for now," said Silas.

"That's a shame," I said, pacing. The cool late afternoon breeze made the leaves flutter, sending some of them sailing off into the building traffic. "Give me a buzz when things improve."

"Will do."

I signed off, wondering now what to do with myself.

The obvious answer would usually be to return to work and make myself useful, but my mind turned instantly to Jennifer. She'd be due a break after the skin graft – that'd be a prime opportunity to get some time alone with her and at least begin to explain. While the weather was mild and pleasant, I could take her for a stroll in one of my favourite haunts; the hospital memorial gardens. We'd find a cosy corner by the roses, and I'd muster up the courage to tell her about Rebecca.

Somehow.

As I turned and made my way around the back of the hospital, I batted my phone against my free hand, trying to drum up ideas. How would a suave git like Silas Griffin summon his lover to the memorial garden for a romantic stroll?

I turned into the rose-entwined archway and slowed my pace, taking in the blooming flower beds and the trees in full leaf.

These gardens were sacred to many families with children in the hospital, especially those who had died. They offered a peaceful place to reflect and remember. I'd always felt calmer for spending time here, surrounded by the beauty of nature – especially against the stark backdrop of the city, where nature gave way to concrete and exhaust fumes.

I stopped by a perfect corner with a stone bench, a place where I could sit with Jen, hold her, and reassure her of my dedication to her. As I took a seat and took out my phone to message her, another thought occurred to me. This could be the perfect location for a proposal; a real one, with a ring I'd chosen for her.

I began typing. *Darling, meet me in the –*

"My god, Wes. I knew I'd find you out here."

My hand gripped my phone so tightly that I could have snapped it in two. Nausea rose up my throat, with an anxiety that made me afraid to look up.

"You look exactly the same, still handsome. Maybe a little more muscular."

My anxiety turned to anger as I glanced up very slowly, my lungs seizing up as I saw her there. She wasn't a nightmare, or a mirage. She was really there, right in front of me, after all these years.

Standing tall in a pair of grey heels and a matching sleeveless dress in a shimmering material, Rebecca looked as graceful and elegant as she ever had. Not that she'd looked that way the very last time I'd seen her – far from it.

Rebecca stood demurely with her hands laced at her front, her long blonde hair tumbling to her waist in elegant waves. Her blue eyes met mine with shadows of the past roiling in them like waves, willing me to remember.

Oh, I remembered.

"You look completely different from the last I saw of you," I said, pocketing my phone. "I seem to remember you hiding behind one of Theo's shirts, with your hair still wet from a romp in our en-suite shower."

Rebecca winced, toying with her fingers. "I should have known you'd still be hurt."

"I was hurt," I said, with more of a bitterness than I'd hoped. "Now I'm relieved."

"Well perhaps you'll be even more relieved to know that Theo and I are divorced," she said, watching me with her icy blue eyes as I got up and walked warily around her, keeping my distance. "I got my comeuppance, Wes."

"I have no feelings about that whatsoever," I said in a short, clipped tone – and I surprised myself by actually meaning it. I really didn't care, even though I had every right to feel victorious.

"I think you do," said Rebecca, challenging me with her stare that went right through me. "A man like you doesn't stop caring."

I chuckled, making her step back in surprise.

"And why would that matter to you? Why would you care what I think now?"

Rebecca licked her lips, frowning down at the lush green grass. "Because I need you to hear that I'm sorry, Wes. I need you to hear it and believe it, completely. If you no longer care, then I'll have wasted my time."

I was aghast at her arrogance. "If all you came here to do is assuage your own guilt now that your marriage has gone to hell in a handcart – "

"That's not all I came here to do," said Rebecca, swaying uncomfortably on the spot.

Anger built inside me, making me pace back and forth. I shook my head with incredulity. "The time for *sorry* was six years ago!"

"I tried, Wes. You didn't want to hear it back then. You did what you always do – you shut yourself down, you cut me out. You wouldn't hear my side of it," said Rebecca, a slight desperation in her voice.

"Because you shacked up with my best friend. I lost *everything*, all at once."

"But you never understood why," she said.

"I didn't want to understand back then, and I don't now," I said, making her turn her head away as if she'd been slapped. "As far as I'm concerned, there can be no reason good enough – "

"You weren't in love with me, Wes. Not then. You were in love with your work, shutting me out, dedicating all your time to everyone but me," said Rebecca.

I laughed, shaking my head at her. "I'm a surgeon. I *have* to put them first. You knew that. For Christ's sake, you couldn't wait for me to graduate. Don't you remember? The rich socialite was going to be married to a surgeon and live happily-ever-after, the envy of her friends."

"I didn't agree to being engaged for more than ten years, wilting away at home on my own for days on end, waiting for you –"

I was being sucked into her void, the pit of despair that I had spent so many years crawling out of – and she'd almost got me. Old patterns set in at an alarming pace. It was as if no time had passed at all, and we were having yet another row that had become common place in the time leading to our breakup.

I wiped a hand over my face, settling over the stubble on my jaw, giving myself a moment to think. Shaking my head, I turned and faced her again. She looked forlorn, wanting. It dawned on me that she was lonely without Theo, and her mind had wandered back to me as the only other person who had cherished her.

"Is the isolation getting to you, Becca?"

Her gaze dropped to the ground, her silken blonde hair forming a curtain around her face. I stepped toward her, brushing it aside. I bent down and leaned in close enough to whisper, eager that she hear what I had to say, close and clear.

"Welcome to the world you two left me in," I whispered.

I held her bare shoulder and she shivered under my touch. I stepped away, pocketing my hands. I turned to leave, but she called after me with a raspy sadness in her voice.

"I heard you're engaged," she said, her voice breaking.

I turned to face her. She looked so small and meek that I almost felt sorry for her; responsible for her, the way I always had been, when my purpose in life was to ensure Rebecca's happiness. Only this time, sorrow was all I felt – any love that there once was between us was long gone.

"I'm glad you came here, Becca. Thank you for this," I said, frowning as I struggled to understand it myself.

"Why?" she asked, in a small voice.

"Because now I know for sure what I really want. Who I really want," I said, with a sudden clarity that made me almost joyful. I couldn't wait to get Jen in my arms, to tell her everything – to show her how desperately I was in love with her.

"Wes, wait – " she called out.

I paused, just briefly.

"I hope she makes you happy, your new fiancé. I – I want you to be happy. I mean that."

I left, then, with the word ringing in my ears: happy. It was a word that hadn't been in my vocabulary for years. It had no place, no worth, and no meaning –

Until Jen.

My bleeper fired off in my pocket, startling me for a moment. An emergency.

I sighed, getting my head back on straight. Jen would have to wait, but at least I knew she'd understand that. She was a fellow doctor, and she knew the score – in fact, she was about to get busier than she'd ever believed possible once she graduated from the surgical programme. Her schedule would be rammed as demand for her grew.

And I would be there, proudly supporting her every step of the way.

CHAPTER FIFTEEN

Jennifer

Connie and I finished up with the application of the fish skin grafts, before winding the dressings over the top. Abbey was too badly burned by a pan of hot water in her school cooking class to manage this procedure without general anaesthetic, but I was confident she would heal up nicely. Dr Ravi, anaesthetist, patiently oversaw her vitals as we closed.

"I'll never get my head around using these slimy things," said Connie, shaking her head as she wound the dressing around Abbey's thigh.

"I think they're pretty cool," I said, laying another silver, shimmering fish skin over the cleaned burn site on Abbey's ankle. "What are we using today?"

"It's tilapia," said Connie. "Glad I'm not

much of a pescatarian."

As we finalised Abbey's dressings, Dr Ravi began to reduce the anaesthetic. Janine would then take Abbey to the recovery room and be there with her when she woke up.

I wrinkled my nose, souring at the thought of Janine being there when anybody woke up. I certainly wouldn't want to see that wasp-chewing sneer when I first opened my eyes.

"So, you and Wes Brookes, huh?" asked Connie, smirking as she tossed her gloves in the orange sanitary bin. "I would never have put the two of you together. Come to think of it, I wouldn't have put him with anyone, given all his...well. His *ways*."

I tossed my gloves and gown and got scrubbing, enjoying the hot water as I soaped up my hands and arms right to the elbows.

"Believe me, I'm as shocked as anyone," I said, my mind instantly going to our mind-blowing, sheet-clawing sex sessions in his beyond-gorgeous apartment. Connie noticed my coy smile and laughed, flashing her bright teeth.

Connie was a little younger than me, with deep mahogany skin that gleamed, and chestnut hair that she almost always wore in a full bun at the nape of her neck. Her appearance was neat and clean, wholly in-keeping with her Christian values. She wore a small, simple silver cross at her throat when she wasn't in surgery, and a silver diamond stud in each ear. She had a purity about her that was charming, but alarming – I wasn't sure how she'd made it to her late twenties without becoming even a little jaded by the world.

I was glad I'd met her and could call her my friend.

Her wholesome smile and simple beauty reminded me that life could be easy, humble, without distraction – just not my life, maybe. Definitely not when I had parents like mine, interfering at every turn.

"You single, Connie?"

She smiled sheepishly, drying off with a bundle of blue paper towels.

"I'm afraid so," she said. "Still waiting for Mr Right."

I took my phone from my pocket and glanced at it, hoping to have heard from Wes – even if he'd only managed to grab a minute or so to send me a kiss. A deep frown took over my face when I found nothing, which even Connie noticed.

"Woah," she said, folding her arms over her chest. "What's got you pouting like a little girl?"

"It's Wes," I said, scowling as I pocketed the phone once more. "I was hoping I'd be seeing him tonight, but it looks like he's still in the thick of it at Royal London."

"See, now *this* is what I'm trying to avoid – going crazy over a man's texts. I could never give them the satisfaction," said Connie. "Next thing you know, you're focusing on them instead of your own life."

She wasn't wrong. I couldn't remember a time when I'd been so focused on another person; in fact, it had cost me relationships that could have gone further if I'd prioritised them. But as we walked out of theatre and made for the break room, my heart gave the familiar flutter of excitement, seeing the hustle and bustle of the department – knowing I was part of something much bigger. Something vital to human survival – children, no less. Who could give that up for anyone?

"You've been an intern here longer than me," I said, grabbing a bottle of water from the staff kitchenette. "Did you...did you ever hear about someone called Rebecca?"

Connie arched an eyebrow. "A surgeon called Rebecca?"

"No, I don't think so. Someone involved with Wes." My dipping tone gave away the relevance of Rebecca to me.

Connie looked up and to the right, thinking. She began to shake her head, and then stopped abruptly, her eyes widening.

"What is it?" I asked in a rush. "Tell me right

now!"

"It's nothing, it's nothing," said Connie, giving me a reassuring glance, "Really, it isn't. Janine did mention that name to me a few times...usually when talking about Wes."

"And? What did she say?"

A big part of me didn't want to know – but another absolutely had to, even though it would give Janine great satisfaction to know it was playing on my mind. Though I no longer saw Janine herself as a threat, she was a clear meddler, and jealous to boot. She seemed like a classic case of *if I can't have him, nobody can.*

"She seemed to despise her. About six months ago, before you joined us, I asked how her day was going – you know, usual chit-chat. She said Rebecca was trying to contact Wes, and that she'd been blocking her attempts. Said she was sick to the back teeth of her," said Connie, shrugging her slim shoulders.

My heart felt it might detach from me and fall to the floor, it ached so hard. My mouth was dry, making me choke as I attempted to speak.

"She said it just like that – Rebecca – as if I was supposed to know who she was talking about," said Connie.

I coughed. "That's because she's significant to Janine. She would have hated her guts for being engaged to Wes."

What frightened me more was the idea that Rebecca had been trying to make contact, which meant she still kept a flame burning for Wes. What other reason could there be? It dawned on me then that if it hadn't been for Janine interfering and blocking her calls, Wes could very well be loved-up with her right now instead of me. He wouldn't have needed me to be his fake fiancé because he would have had the real thing.

Was that why he refused to talk about her? Was he really, truly still in love with her?

A faintness came over me, the room swaying. Connie leapt forward, holding me by the elbow as she steadied me.

"Hey, what's going on with you?" she asked, concern in her deep brown eyes. "Have you been overdoing it?"

"Are you on-call tonight, Connie? Because I could really use something to drink," I said, feeling limp and woozy.

Connie wrapped an arm around my waist, supporting me. Her gentle demeanour had a calming effect on me, even though my heart was racing.

"I think I could manage a drink or two," she said, helping me along. "For you."

♥

Next door to Gina's on the high street was an upmarket bar called Dickens, serving cocktails and fine wines. The interior was black with plush plum-coloured booths. Enormous pen and ink illustrations from the works of Charles Dickens took up the walls from floor to ceiling in strategic spaces. As we took a booth and looked at the menu, I could see the Artful Dodger doffing his oversized hat on one wall, and Miss Haversham glaring in her decaying wedding dress by the ladies toilets.

I relaxed a little, but only a little.

"I'm in the mood for one of these speciality cocktails," said Connie, scanning the menu. "Charlie's Tipple – that's cute. It's a mint julep."

"I'll have a Nancy – looks like a fancy gin," I said.

Connie clucked her tongue, playfully admonishing me with a waggle of her finger. "Gin makes you weep."

"I'm surprised you even drink at all, with that cross you wear," I said. "I figured you were more of a...curling up with your cocoa kind of person."

Connie laughed, batting me in the shoulder. I smiled, feeling my mood lightening already.

"You have to know how to relax a little in life, or you'll be bogged down with all the misery. There's always something to smile about. I don't think Jesus minds if I have a little cocktail," said Connie.

There was always something to smile about

– and I knew, at least, that my fears with Wes and Rebecca were purely speculation at this point. I was jealous, scared, and my mind was working overtime. When our drinks arrived, sparkling with ice and lime and a glass stirrer each, we knocked them together.

"Cheers!"

We were midway through our second round when my heart stopped. There at the bar was Janine, perched on a bar stool, sipping a Bloody Mary.

"Oh god, of all the places – do you want to leave? Go somewhere else?" Connie's hand felt my arm, reassuring me.

"No," I said finally, watching Janine sip her cocktail on her own. I found myself almost feeling sorry for her, and not for the first time. "No, we'll stay here. She'll keep her distance."

But as the words left my mouth, Janine spotted me, a triumphant grin spreading across her face. She hopped down off the bar stool and picked up her Bloody Mary, making her way towards us.

"You were saying?" asked Connie.

I straightened, ready to tell Janine exactly where she could go – in the most professional way possible, of course. Although the gin cocktail was working its magic already, giving me a delightful buzz, I was determined not to make a fool of myself.

"Got something I need to show you," she said. "It's not pretty."

"Whatever it is, I'm not interested, Janine," I said.

"You will be." She slid her phone across the table in front of me. As my eyes dropped to the horror that greeted me, she flicked her finger across the screen, showing me photo after photo, until I wanted to throw up.

At first I thought she'd taken a photo of me, for the person in the picture resembled me so much that it confused me. When had I ever stood with Wes in a garden like that? And I didn't own a grey sleeveless dress, or those killer heels.

My hand shot to my mouth as I gasped, realising it wasn't me at all. It was her.

Rebecca.

"Taken just a couple of hours ago," said Janine. "I was taking a break in the memorial garden and heard their voices. Sorry to be the bearer of bad news, but I did try to warn you."

I tried to make sense of it, though the bile rising in my throat made it impossible to think straight.

"Come on, those pictures could have been taken any time," said Connie, though she didn't sound too convinced. "He's at the Royal London

Hospital right now."

"Look at the time stamps," said Janine. "Look at what he's wearing."

My stomach roiled angrily, a headache clustering behind my eyes. As Janine continued flicking through the photos, she paused on one that nearly made me vomit on the spot. Wes was leaning in, his hand delicately brushing the hair aside from Rebecca's face as she shied away from him. It looked like he was kissing her.

The man I loved had met with his ex – the one who got away – in a rose garden and kissed her. Worse, he'd told me he was away on surgery to cover his tracks.

"Just think, while you were working on the skin grafts, he was out there with her, right under your nose," said Janine. "How does it feel to be replaced?"

Her words hit me like a hammer to the head. I shoved her aside and ran for the ladies' bathroom, retching as fluid filled my mouth. As I burst through the toilet door, Miss Haversham eyed me with her pitying gaze, her expression embittered but unsurprised.

It was as if she was telling me I should have known this would happen. That I should have suspected as much.

I'd been given fair warning.

CHAPTER SIXTEEN

Wesley

When I finally left theatre, it was late. Jen would have gone home by now.

Cursing under my breath, I realised it would be too late to sweep her away to my apartment and explain everything to her about Rebecca. Seeing her in the garden and feeling the absence of love had given me the shake-up I'd needed, forcing me to really look at my priorities.

Jen was right; she did deserve to know everything.

She was the woman I loved, and it was high time I shared my past with her. No longer would I be self-centred, self-interested, keeping myself locked up for fear of rejection. Janine's words still rang in my ears; that I used people to prop myself up, to bring comfort to me, while I gave little consideration to them.

I wasn't a fan of hers right now by any means, despite her years of service to the department – but I couldn't ignore the truth. I knew it was true, because it hurt me to think of it. Only a harsh reality could have that effect on me.

As I entered the cavernous atrium and made my way toward the exit, a delicate ditty drifted to my ears, letting those thoughts fade away momentarily. I smiled, seeing one of our janitors playing on the donated piano. Placed before the sculptural fountain – a fairytale depiction of a little girl and her baby brother looking at fish in a stream, which then became the water feature – I had long been meaning to spend some time there. Maybe play a little tune, though I loathed the way people crowded around and watched me while I played.

I could do it for Jen, knowing how she'd loved it when I unknowingly played her favourite song – that moment which had given us both a feeling of destiny.

Checking my phone, it concerned me that Jen hadn't left any messages.

Of course, I thought – considerate, lovely Jennifer had let me be, expecting that I was in surgery at Royal London. I would explain to her that the surgery was cancelled, and that I'd stayed here after all – and then I'd take her to my place, and tell her I'd seen Rebecca. I'd tell her everything, start to finish.

And then I'd make it up to her, teasing her gorgeous little body all night, until she fell asleep in my arms.

I called her. I called again. A deep disappointment fell over me when Jen didn't answer.

I sent her a text instead, wishing her sweet dreams, and made for my car. I would sleep without her and see her in the morning.

Knowing that I would be greeted by her face brought me the peace I needed to drift off, where I would usually be too buzzed from a late emergency.

♥

I waited, eagerly pacing, while Janine wrote up the day's schedule on the board. I had two mugs of surgeon's tea ready for us on the nurses' station – I knew that'd make Jen smile. When Janine saw that I'd come in early and made our own tea, she'd rolled her eyes, and hadn't said two words to me since.

"Where is my paper schedule, Janine?" I asked.

She paused her writing and gave me a scathing look. "You can print your own, can't you?"

I studied her face, noticing something was

off.

"Do you have anything to say to me, Janine?" I asked in a clipped tone.

"Not at all," she said, an aubergine-tinted smile spreading across her face.

I raised my eyebrows. "I don't think much of your new lipstick," I said.

"I don't think much of your new girlfriend," she said.

I balled my fists as she smirked, knowing I'd walked right into that one. It saddened me that my relationship with her – someone so vital to my practice – had gone royally south, but it angered me even more to hear her speak of Jen that way.

"I'm sorry – I meant, your new *fiancé*," she added.

Sighing, I took a gulp of my lukewarm tea. I couldn't correct her without creating yet more drama, so I let it go. Besides, I enjoyed the thought of Jen as my real fiancé. Where the heck *was* Jen?

"I'll be in my office, printing out the schedule," I said. "Tell my wife-to-be where to find me when she gets here."

Janine's smirk dropped as I turned and left, wondering if I could even remember how to use the dreaded printer. Unsurprisingly, the thing jammed, clawing up too much paper – and after battling with that, the screen announced it was out of toner, too.

Cursing, I turned in time to see Jen walk past my office at speed, her lips pressed firmly together, her mouth set as steel.

"Jen!" I called out, hurrying after her – but she kept going, her back to me. "Darling, what's – "

She span, hissing under her breath. "Do *not* darling me!"

Baffled, I put my hand to the back of my neck as she stormed off. I hurried after her once again, keeping my voice low but urgent.

"Jen, you're going to have to fill me in here – "

"I know you were with Rebecca. *I know.*"

Jen turned and fled again, marching off toward the wings as if she had somewhere to be – but she was supposed to be with me.

"Uh, Dr Brookes?"

I turned, shaking my head, to find Dr Bingham standing behind me, clutching a bundle of notes.

"What is it, Connie?"

She gulped, looking uneasy. "Dr Hurst asked to swap clinic with me, today. She said she had some important patients to check-in on."

"She's got multiple surgeries, for Christ's sake. She can't just – "

"She swapped those with me, too. She's

asked to scrub-in on orthopaedics today."

I gritted my teeth, realising I'd given Jen far too much freedom – part of our agreement that she was happily exploiting now. Then a nasty feeling clawed at my insides, wondering if she might cut and run altogether, jumping ship to another department.

"She's avoiding me," I said lamely, clawing my hand through my hair.

Connie's eyebrows lifted, looking at me as if I'd said something incredibly stupid.

"Is it any *wonder*?"

I frowned, noting that she seemed to know something I didn't. I ushered her along with me, determined to get to the bottom of this.

♥

As I paced outside theatre, waiting for Jen, I spotted Janine.

"If I could sack you on the spot, I would," I said, glaring at her.

She laughed, sunny, as if she didn't have a care in all the world.

"Good thing I don't actually work for you," she said, and she wasn't wrong – the nursing team were an entirely separate entity with their own governance. "Maybe I should put in a complaint about you for abusing my time and resources."

"You *are* supposed to assist me. We're

supposed to be a *team*."

Connie had – mercifully – filled me in. Janine knew very-well that I hadn't kissed Rebecca, and that those photos only told part of the story – a very damning part. I was surprised at how wicked she could be.

"Well I'd love to know how team spirit fits in with your blatant favouritism, Dr Brookes," she said. "See you soon."

I frowned, wondering what she meant by that – *see you soon*. If I had my way I'd never see the vindictive witch again at this point.

I was so busy seething at Janine that Jen almost managed to get by me, heading straight for the lifts.

"Jen! Stop, please listen to me – "

"I don't want to hear it," she muttered, hammering at the call button with her thumb. When it didn't arrive instantly, she made for the stairs. I was glad – it would give us at least some level of privacy.

Hurrying after her, Jen took the stairs briskly, eager to get away from me – but I wasn't about to let her go. As we reached the first landing, I grabbed her around the wrist.

"Get off of me!"

"Please, Jen, for god's sake, listen to me. I did *not* lie to you!"

Her eyes narrowed as she sneered. "Give it a rest, Wes."

"I'm telling the truth – "

"Really? Because it looked a lot like you lied to me about your whereabouts, met up with your ex who looks *freakishly* similar to me, the woman who pretended to be your fiancé for the sake of your parents –"

" – she doesn't look a bit like you."

Jen tossed her head and laughed. "Please, Wes, just stop –"

"She doesn't have your crystal blue eyes, your voluptuous beautiful body, your kind smile, your sharp mind, that happy, lovely way about you – she has *nothing* that you have. She's a sulking bore who spends more time pampering herself than she does thinking about others. You've dedicated your *life* to helping people. You're the only woman I've ever known who could really understand who I am and what I do."

Something I said seemed to give Jen pause, allowing me to speak. I saw tears filling her eyes.

"Then why did you kiss her?"

"That was nothing more than a strategic angle. I've no interest in kissing that woman any more than I have interest in swallowing a handful of thumb-tacks," I said.

"Then what were you doing, getting so close

to her?"

I closed my eyes. "I was asking her how it feels to...to be alone. I was a bastard, Jen."

"Then she really did break your heart," said Jen, her voice faltering.

I could see it was tearing her up – I could only imagine how I would feel if I saw Jen getting close to another man like that. Just the thought of it made my teeth clench. Jen shook her head, as if deciding something in her own mind, and pushed through the double-doors and into the hallway.

"Jen, wait – please, let's go somewhere private and talk this out. We'll go to my apartment, have a beautiful dinner – "

"You still lied about Royal London," said Jen, walking briskly in the direction of the break room. The handover was taking place, with the oncoming staff huddling around the nurses' station. I kept my voice low, keen that nobody else noticed our drama.

"I did *not* lie about Royal London!"

"Please, Wes. You made plans to meet her there in the garden and you used Royal London as a cover story for me," said Jen, rolling her eyes.

"That surgery was cancelled and I was called to an emergency soon after – Rebecca just found me there!"

Jen laughed again, incredulously. I realised

how ridiculous I sounded in that moment – what were the odds of Rebecca being on the hospital grounds exactly when I was, when I was due to leave the building?

"You expect me to believe she just bumped into you?"

I groaned. "I don't know how she found me, Jen, but she did."

Jen reached the break room door, resting her hand on it to push. "Right, and what are the chances of that happening? About as likely as – "

"SURPRISE!"

Confetti rained down on us to the blaring noise of party-blowers.

Blinking, we looked around at the ordinarily bland break room now decorated with streamers and clusters of silver and white balloons. Swags lined the two small tables, which had been pushed together and covered in a white linen cloth. A buffet had been laid out on top and, in the centre, a large white cake with a glittering love-heart topper.

"This…looks like an engagement party," Jen muttered.

We stood side by side, gob-smacked, as our colleagues applauded, whooping and cheering. I felt almost light-headed as I saw the enormous banner tacked up at the window – *Congratulations Wesley and Jennifer*!

Janine was standing by a table crudely laden with glasses and bottles of sparkling wine. She popped a bottle and poured the contents into two glasses with long stems, before handing one each to me and Jen.

"*Enjoy*, you two," she said, with a smirk.

CHAPTER SEVENTEEN

Jennifer

"What the heck do we do?" I hissed at Wes, glancing uneasily at all the people waiting to congratulate us.

"We smile," he said, grinning in a false way that would have ordinarily made me dissolve into a fit of giggles. "And we look like we're having a good time."

"I'm going to enjoy this champagne, I know that much," I said, greeting the first oncoming colleague who wanted to shake my hand.

As Wes was distracted with a group of his colleagues, I searched the room, looking for Connie. When I found her, she was nibbling a carrot dipped in her plate of hummus.

"Are you having fun?"

Connie shrugged. "It's a party! Why, what's

wrong?"

"Everything's wrong," I said, tears still pooling in my eyes when I thought about those photos. "And where the hell is that music coming from?"

"Did he tell you, yet? It was all a big misunderstanding. It's just Janine interfering out of jealousy, that's all. Ignore her. Don't give her the satisfaction," said Connie.

"But what about the lies – what about the fact he said he was in Royal London when he damn-well wasn't?"

"Ah – I wondered the same thing. He told me it was cancelled, right? So after our first surgery today, I had a look on the computer – and what do you know? His call-out *was* cancelled, to be rescheduled at a later date," said Connie, stabbing the air with her carrot stick.

I gulped. "So he really was supposed to be at RL?"

"His story completely checks out," said Connie. "I think you can trust the guy, Jen. It's *her* you can't trust."

We both let our eyes wander to Janine, who raised her glass to us. I wondered if she knew that mine and Wes' engagement had been false all along, and just wanted to embarrass us – or worse, that this was some psychotic self-punishment, where she made Wes see how much he was hurting her.

As I made my way to her, I could see I was right – her smug face was hiding the tears that were prickling her eyes. She was in pain, gripped by envy, and she'd wanted to make me feel that way too. The party was just her way of rubbing it in at my weakest point, when I would be freshly devastated by the photos of Wes and Rebecca.

"You think this party bothers me?"

Janine sneered over the rim of her glass. "Just rubbing a little salt in the wounds. Now you can know how I feel, having to face everybody day in, day out. I practically washed that man's feet, I was such a slave to him – and for what? For him to become a simpering mess over *you*?"

I lowered my head, uncomfortable to see how much she was hurting. Despite my anger at the multiple attempts she'd made to sabotage our relationship, I couldn't help but see the truth – she had failed, and now she was only hurting herself.

I remembered Connie's words, about how Janine had been fielding desperate phone calls from Rebecca six months before I joined the department.

"It was you, wasn't it – you told Rebecca when and where to find Wes. You wanted them to just casually *bump* into each other and for all the old sparks to start flying," I said, shaking my head at her. "*Anything* to ensure that he and I couldn't be together."

Janine smiled, a bitterness interrupting her dark beauty. "I even invited her to this party. I guess she was too scared to show."

"She didn't show because he rejected her, the same way he rejected you."

Janine winced, and I felt triumphant. Surely, finally, she would see that all she was doing was spreading her own pain around, drawing others into it? She folded her arms and downed her drink, her eyes glancing toward the drinks table for another one.

My eyes found Wes amongst his huddle of surgical buddies from other departments, even other hospitals. A sudden urge to show Janine came over me. An urge to show them all that he wanted me.

I marched up to Wes and tapped him on the shoulder, the crowd around him taking a step back. Wes looked disoriented as he turned to me, and then surprised. He paused momentarily, his green eyes studying mine, taking me in.

"Are you all right? Are you – "

I interrupted his sentence by kissing him, my hands cupping his face before I threw my arms around his neck. Our guests began to cat-call; someone told us to get a room. Their gentle jeering turned to full-on wolf-whistling and applause as Wes lifted me into his arms and dipped me over his arm, kissing me long and deep. My body went limp as I filled my hands with his hair, my eyes closed as a sensual longing came over me, even despite our audience.

As he planted me back down on the ground, our eyes met, and I wanted to melt into him; I wanted to be back at his apartment, my hands roaming his hard body as his hips rocked me to orgasm.

"Let me get my jacket, and we'll get out of here," Wes whispered, brushing my cheek with the backs of his fingers.

"Gladly," I said, knowing my face was pink and flushed with desire.

As I watched Wes make for the bunk room where he'd left his jacket, someone I didn't recognise appeared at my side.

"Jen. I'm Gabriel Grant, orthopaedic surgeon. I noticed you in the OR today – I was across the way in OR2."

I looked him up and down, wondering how I'd managed not to notice a man like him wandering around the hospital. Standing at least 6"5, he was enormous, his shoulders and torso as wide and girthy as a tree trunk. He had lightly tanned skin and glossy black locks that fell in layers almost to his shoulders, with piercing blue eyes that were even paler than mine.

He grinned devilishly in a way that made

my heart leap – not because he was my type exactly, but because his dominating form, and the intense sexuality in that naughty grin of his, was too arresting to ignore. I found myself blushing, not knowing where to look. He wore a tight-fitting pale blue shirt that matched his eyes, and black trousers with a belt that drew attention to his lean waist.

"I – " I cleared my throat, finding it hard to speak. "I've never seen you around here before."

"I'm new to Sacred Heart. Fancy a dance?"

"Oh, no, I – " But it was too late – he took my hand and span me, before pulling me close to his large, hard body. He swayed and rocked me, forcing my hand on his hip while he held my other hand aloft. He twirled me again, and this time I laughed, enjoying the playful way he commanded my movements.

As he pulled me in close to him again, his lips found my ear. "You know, if Brookes doesn't turn out to be any good for you..."

I laughed, tapping him gently on his hard chest. "I can assure you, he's everything I want and more."

Gabriel cocked a dark eyebrow, accepting my remark with a smirk. But he wasn't letting up; his grip was tight on my waist, apparently enjoying the control of forcing me to dance. It was beginning to get too much.

He lowered his mouth to my ear again. His silken, snake-like voice gave me shivers. It was sexy, if a little sinister.

"You wouldn't be able to point out which one of these ladies is Connie Bingham, would you?"

"What do you want with Connie?" I asked, scared that he might be looking to prey on someone for an easy lay – and Connie was definitely not it. The thought of him getting his large hands on delicate, church-going Connie made me almost afraid for her.

"Relax," he said, giving me that devil's smile again with his pointed incisors. "I'm not looking to defile your friends. Connie's going to be my intern – I'll be leading her from now on in orthopaedics."

"Oh," I said faintly, unable to decide whether that made Connie lucky or not. I turned my head and found Connie, standing in a group with a handful of nurses and our intern colleagues. She was laughing, enjoying the conversation with a soft drink in her hand. Her necklace caught the light, glinting.

"That's her – the one with the cross at her neck."

Gabriel's hands dropped to my waist as he took in Connie's image. She was wearing a simple outfit of tight black drainpipe trousers and a scoop-neck top to match. It highlighted her trim figure and narrow waist; simple and elegant,

Connie could make the plainest clothes look expensive.

I looked up at Gabriel and felt anxiety ripple through me as his eyes darkened, his gaze absolutely fixed on Connie. His lips parted slightly as if he'd just witnessed something spectacular and was awe-struck. Connie, as if sensing eyes on her, glanced our way – and was equally transfixed by Gabriel.

"Shall I introduce – "

My words were rudely cut off by Gabriel staggering backwards and away from me as Wes, his expression furious and his shoulders squared, shoved Gabriel hard in the chest. Gabriel recovered quickly, squaring back up to Wes, his expression twisting to one of malevolence.

"Keep your hands off of her," said Wes, his voice low and stern.

People were beginning to notice something was going on, and became silent. I shifted on the spot, blushing furiously and...what the heck was going on? I realised I'd become moist between the legs at seeing Wes so protective of me – dare I say, possessive of me. It wasn't something I'd ever encourage, but seeing him angered by another man's touch was doing wild things to me.

I was tense as my eyes flitted between Wes and Gabriel, afraid that a fight was about to break out.

Thankfully, Gabriel's intense glare melted away to his wicked grin. Despite being taller and larger than Wes, he threw his hands up in the air as a show of backing down.

"It's all good," he said, stepping away. "I was just taking her for a spin on the dance floor, that's all."

Wes glared at him as if he still wanted to thump him, and I could see a vein straining in his neck. His fists were clenched. If I didn't get him away soon, hell could break loose. I was grateful when Gabriel was the first to turn and walk away, smiling wryly as he picked up a piece of popcorn shrimp from the buffet table and popped it in his mouth.

Wes' fiery eyes turned on me, his usual verdant irises somehow darker.

"How could you let him touch you like that?"

I raised my eyebrows, appalled. "Wait, you're not serious?"

"He had his hands all over you."

After all the grief I'd taken with Janine and Rebecca together, I found myself desperately fighting the urge to laugh.

"*You're* jealous?"

"Of course I am. I'm – I'm fucking furious," said Wes, hissing under his breath. His hands were on my elbows, holding me close to him, but with an aggression I wasn't used to. I found myself getting hotter, the little nub above my moistening sex pulsing with longing.

I wanted to say, *now you know how it feels, buddy*, but what I said instead was much better.

"Why don't you take it out on me?" I whispered, looking up at him.

His eyes narrowed and a flush crept up his neck as his hands tightened at my elbows. Suddenly his hand was in mine, pulling me out of the room and into the short corridor between us and the bunk room. When I realised he was taking me to bed, right in the middle of the party, my nipples tightened to hard buds.

Wes barely had the door closed behind us before he was tugging my blouse over my head and tearing off my bra. He lunged greedily at my breasts, cupping them in both hands and squeezing them rhythmically. I panted and gasped at the sudden onslaught of pleasure as his lips clamped around one nipple and then the other, his tongue rolling them as he drew on them in a suckling motion.

Wes backed me toward the lower bunk and threw me down, before pulling off my shoes and trousers in two swift movements. As he unbuckled his trousers and let his enormous, beautiful cock spring free, I squirmed, impossibly wet just from the sight of him.

The bed dipped and the springs strained as he climbed directly on top of me, going straight between my legs. He parted them with his strong thighs and lifted me under the knees, opening me. My breasts heaved with every breath I took, my sex pulsing and throbbing for him.

The roller-coaster of highs and lows I'd been on in just the last few days came to a peak in my mind, intensifying the experience. He wanted me – no other woman. Me. And the rock-hard cock nudging at my opening proved it.

"Fuck me, Wes. Make me yours. *Show me* I'm yours."

Wes grunted and rammed his cock into me, sliding in directly as my wetness aided his passage. He propped himself on his elbows and fucked me to get in deep, before hooking his right arm under my leg and holding it up higher. No matter how deep he got, it wasn't enough for either of us. I cried his name as we rutted, both rabid with ecstasy in the race to climax. I clutched his shoulder blades as he muttered curse words and pummelled me, his hips so rhythmic and teasing that his pubis hit the sweetest, most desirable spot – my aching, pulsing clitoris. With every thump I was closer to coming, clawing at him, crying desperately for him to get me there.

As I mounted that peak and shattered, I wailed into the crook of his neck, before throwing my head back and crying out with every wave of orgasm that rolled deliciously over and through me.

At my sounds of pleasure, Wes went hard as a piston, and as my own cries of pleasure faded, he reached his climax. His cock was hard as marble as he thrust deep and abruptly stopped, his pained face giving way to a sweet vulnerability as he began to pulse inside me. With every pulse came a gush of thick, warm cum, coating my insides. He gave one final nudge, right under my womb, before collapsing on top of me.

I held him close, wrapping my arms and legs tight around him. We panted and sighed, our skin as equally bathed in a balm of sweat. His hand found my hair and stroked it away from my face as he lazily kissed me, smiling and sated.

I snuggled as close to him as I could possibly get, tucking inside his arms with my head close under his chin.

"I think I'm going to cut my hair," I said, as Wes stroked it and let it fall between his fingers.

"Don't you dare cut any of this beautiful hair," he said, tipping my head back as he playfully bit my earlobe. "Why would you think of doing that?"

"You know why," I said, looking up at him.

Wes sighed, squeezing me tighter around the shoulders.

"Jen, come on – "

"Please, just put me out of my misery, once and for all – so we can move on *together* from this."I took a deep breath. "Did you choose me, initially, because I looked similar to Rebecca?"

"No," said Wes, firmly, and without even waiting a beat. "And I already told you, you two look nothing alike."

I screwed up my face in confusion. "She's my height without her heels, she's got long blonde hair, blue eyes..."

"She does not look like *you*. Not to me. Do I look like every green-eyed man with blonde hair who happens to be about 6"2?"

I laughed, then. "No, definitely not. But there is a resemblance, Wes. I'm not comfortable with it – and it's worse if you don't admit it."

He rolled his eyes, wiping a hand over his face as if exasperated. "I did note a similarity, yes. All right. But that wasn't what attracted me, and it's certainly not what made me fall in love with you."

"Subconsciously?"

"I don't make decisions subconsciously, I make them consciously after considering the options thoroughly."

"So I should be pleased, then, that you have a type – maybe I should find that reassuring," I said, mulling over the pros and cons with a hint of sarcasm. "Who were your other options?"

The feeling of Wes' fingers massaging my labia before dipping inside me made my mouth drop open in a gasp.

"I wouldn't usually ask, darling," he said, running kisses down my jaw and neck as his fingers slid deeper inside me. "But please stop talking."

♥

I sat on the edge of Wes' rumpled bed, naked and sated and serene, with the London skyline providing me with a beautiful scene to gaze out on. The red flickering light of a passing passenger plane winked between the Gherkin and the Cheesegrater as it sailed along.

Finally, Wes had told me every grizzly detail of his relationship with Rebecca. By the time he'd remembered more than ten years of a dying engagement, culminating in the discovery of Rebecca in the arms of his best friend Theo, Wes was destroyed. His body tense, his expression pained, his voice a whisper. He still, partly, blamed himself for neglecting her; for not loving her the way he'd promised her he would. He told me of his anguish, returning to his parents' home, his only sanctuary away from the world. How he'd thrown himself into his work and gradually become embittered, knowing that his schedules and routines were the only consistent thing in his life that he had left to rely on.

Janine had formed some part of that, meeting his needs in the workplace. And then he'd met me, and his softer side felt safe enough, finally, to show its face after years of recovery from heartbreak.

There was only one way I knew to show my gratitude to him for sharing his pain with me. I soothed it with my body, our souls connecting as we kissed and writhed on the bed, forgetting it all on waves of mutual pleasure.

There came the humming sound of the shower running. Wes appeared in the bathroom doorway, totally naked with his large, beautiful cock on full display. He gripped the top of the door frame and relaxed against it, giving me a view of his rippling stomach muscles and Adonis belt that made my womb clench to look at them.

"The gym any good in this apartment building?" I asked wryly, looking him up and down.

He grinned, his hair a tousled mess from our lovemaking. "It must be, I use it every morning. You can join me tomorrow, if you like."

"Mm," I considered. "I'm torn. On one hand I can't think of anything more horrible than waking up early to use the gym – on the other hand, seeing you getting all hot and sweaty..."

"We can get hot and sweaty together," he said. As he said it, I saw his cock thicken and twitch, stirred by the delicious mental image he conjured. "Coming in the shower?"

"I plan to," I said, making him laugh. He turned and I heard the creak of the shower door.

My phone buzzed, shimmying along the bed spread. I hung my head and groaned when I saw the name. Ugh, anyone but her.

Ever the dutiful daughter, I answered.

"Hello, mother," I said glumly.

"What's that tone for? You haven't even heard what I have to say yet," said mum.

"Something tells me it won't be good."

"Well, that's up to you."

I frowned, standing and pacing the plush peach-coloured carpet. "What's that supposed to mean?"

"Your father and I heard there was an engagement party hosted in the break room of the plastics department. You've completely disregarded everything I've said, haven't you? Any surgeon who dates his interns is bad news."

"It just happened, mother – neither of us planned to fall in love. But we have," I said defiantly. "And you need to get used to me making my own decisions."

My mother's laughter made me hold the phone away from my face in disgust.

"We'll see how good you are at making your

own decisions, Jennifer," she said. "Your father is so sick about it that he's barely been able to digest a meal. I, as you know, am not that soft. This is for your own good."

"What is?"

Mum sighed. "If you go ahead with this engagement and get married to Wesley Brookes, your father and I will disown and disinherit you. It will kill us to do it, but we're not about to give away your birth right to some charlatan who preys on his own students."

A coldness came over me, then, and I nearly dropped the phone. It seemed like an age before I could speak, frozen as I was to the spot.

"Disinherit I can live with, mum – but disown? Is that a sick joke?"

"I wish it was. It all seems like a joke to me," said mum. "But you have a choice to make. You can go back to the way things were before, or you can carry on with this man and lose everything."

"You want to completely write me out of the will and never see me again?"

"Nobody wants that, Jennifer, but it's the only way you'll learn what's really important," said mum in a dark, flat tone of voice.

After my now-decades of making every decision with their approval in mind, this was a brutal punch to the stomach. Years upon years of acting in their best interests instead of my own, of suppressing every whim or difference of opinion, had all been for nothing. My parents still had absolutely no respect for me and, I realised, never would.

A painful grief swept over me, my tears falling down toward my bare feet. I couldn't even muster up my own voice to speak. I was a child again, admonished by my parents for some small infraction, wondering why they despised their only daughter.

"You stand to lose tens of millions, Jennifer – not to mention your own flesh and blood. You've never been one for independence, dear. You've always sought our approval. You were a smart girl in some ways, but painfully naive in others – to the point that your father and I didn't know what to do with you. You're an adult now. You've got an adult decision to make," said mum.

I stifled a sob, knowing they didn't deserve any of my tears, but unable to hold them back regardless. The pain was too much; the sunken losses too much to bear. They were my parents, and they still only saw me as little band kid Jen with an ill-fitting uniform, embarrassing them as I walked on stage with all the other children. Jilted Jen who couldn't even keep an arsehole like Graham. I was still a nuisance they had to put up with, unable to live up to their expectations of me.

By the time I felt able to respond, I realised the phone was dead. Mum had ended the call.

"J-e-n," sang Wesley from the bathroom.

I made my way to the shower, hugging my own arms. As I stepped into the steam, Wes folded me into his hot embrace, enveloping me in his love. I broke down instantly, overwhelmed by the comfort and understanding that radiated from every pore in his body.

"What's going on?" he asked, cupping my head in his hands. "Tell me."

"My parents," I said, barely managing to choke those two words out before I shuddered and dissolved into more tears.

Wes asked nothing, only held me to him.

Then he soaped up his hands and began to caress me, turning me gently in his embrace. As he washed me, I cried, relaxing into his arms and letting him do all the work. He washed my body, taking care around my buttocks and between my thighs, and then worked shampoo into my hair. His fingers massaged my scalp, before he drew them down my head and neck and finished with a massage on my shoulders.

Once we were rinsed off, he helped me out of the shower and wrapped me in a large, fluffy peach-coloured towel, warm and comforting from the heated towel rack on the wall. Wes rubbed himself down with an identical towel and tucked it in around his waist. Then he scooped me up in his arms and planted me in the plush armchair by the window, where he towel-dried my hair and ran a wide-toothed comb through my locks.

All the while I sniffed and cried, stricken by grief. I wasn't yet sure, really, what I was crying for specifically – the news that I didn't have to see them again should have been a dream come true, frankly. Why, then, did I feel such loss?

Wes tucked us up in bed and turned out the light, spooning me with his arm holding me snug and close, our legs tangled up beneath the duvet.

Even as Wes' breathing became heavier and he began to softly snore, I cried, nursing the loss that I could neither understand nor explain.

CHAPTER EIGHTEEN

Wesley

At a time when we should have been blissfully happy and in love, Jen had withdrawn and become a shell of herself. Days passed in my apartment, where we worked between our lovemaking sessions and retreated back home the moment we could. But Jen was becoming more detached, her eyes never quite meeting mine as her mind took her elsewhere.

I wanted to drive to her parents' place and have it out with them – to tell them what a disgrace they were for putting her in a position that nobody would ever want to be in. To be forced to choose, no matter how tenuous the connection, was a cruelty that I could never imagine my own parents dealing me.

I glanced at Jen now in the passenger seat, slumped and staring nonchalantly out of the window. How could they treat her so abysmally, when she'd lived every moment of her life with their approval as her goal? Didn't they have any love for the beautiful young woman they created – seemingly despite their best efforts to sabotage her?

It didn't make any sense, but then, neither did anything right now. As we drove toward her flat-share in Islington, I firmed my decision in my mind. It was the only right thing to do.

I pulled up at the curbside and killed the engine.

Jen gave me a weak smile as she felt for the door handle. "I'll only be a moment – I'll just grab a few essentials. My toothbrush, my hair brush. You could come in and meet my flat mates if you like, although some of them will have been on night shifts – "

Her voice was dull, lacking her usual vibrancy or nuance in tone.

"Darling, listen to me," I said, taking her hand in mine. Fear entered her eyes as she registered my tone – the only real emotion I'd seen from her in days, except for when I brought her to orgasm, or when she was crying.

"I can't stand this for another minute," I said. "Seeing you like this – it's painful. I know this is destroying you inside."

"Wes, please don't do this," she said in a

meek voice, tears rolling down her cheeks.

"Listen to me, beautiful – please, trust me. I didn't bring you here just to gather a few things and then come back to hide at my apartment. I brought you here so I...so I could leave you here."

"What?" she whispered, cupping her hands over her mouth to hide a sob.

"This is *not* me leaving you. This is me being responsible and doing what's best for you."

"You do *not* know what's best for me!" she cried.

I grabbed her hands and held them, rubbing the backs of them with my thumbs.

"Listen to me. I want you to spend some time alone and think – really, really think – about how you want to deal with this. Your parents have been pretty damn clear about their end of things – "

"I hate them," she said, almost spitting the words. "I won't give in to them."

I kissed the backs of her hands, smiling at her. It was music to my ears – but still, I had to do what needed to be done, for her sake. No, for our sake – for the integrity of our relationship going forward.

"Then you need to be absolutely sure of that. You can't be certain while I'm in the way, distracting you."

"Bullshit. You're sick to death of me crying and you want out, right?"

"You can't believe that, angel. You know me better than that. I would take you whatever way I could have you. I'd keep you for myself in my apartment, and I'd drive you to work and love you and your little body every moment I could around that. But it wouldn't be right."

She groaned, tossing her head back against the head rest.

"Fuck that," she said.

"If I don't handle this the right way now, it'll plague me for the rest of our days together. Would you want that?"

Jen furiously clutched her hair in bunches at her scalp. "I'm *telling you*, I don't want anything to do with them."

"And I'm telling you that it isn't that simple, and you know it," I said, praying that she would see things my way and understand.

"These are your parents. Whether rightly or wrongly, you have spent a lifetime dedicated to their approval of you. If I let you walk away from them now, you will never know with all honesty just how much I influenced you. It mightn't happen today or tomorrow, but it will, and you'll ask yourself whether I coerced you, or whether you made too-hasty a decision. I'll piss you off and in a moment of anger, you'll fire back at me that you lost everything for me."

"I wouldn't ever say that," Jen bit back.

I swallowed hard, knowing this was partly supposition – but knowing, too, that I was experienced enough in life to know how these hasty decisions could backfire. Rebecca had said similar in our arguments – that she'd waited and sacrificed for me – and it had led to our destruction. I could accept that now.

But losing Jen was something I wasn't willing to even contemplate.

"I want no barriers in our way, darling. When we argue in the future – and we will, when things get stressful and tough and we can't stand the sight of one another – I want you to remember that you *chose* me. Not that you *lost* for me, or gave everything *up* for me," I said. "Then, you'll remember why you love me – and I'll remember why I love you, so dearly that it hurts. We'll know without a doubt that we chose one another; that we weren't forced together by circumstance."

Jen furiously wiped the tears from her cheeks.

"Then why does this feel like yet another horrible rejection?" she asked.

"Because you're low, and you need me – and my god, Jen, I want to be there for you. If I didn't think I was preventing you from getting better, then you know I'd wrap you in my arms and never let go. I'd never let the world get to you again. I'd block out every cruel word said, especially by your parents, and I'd be everything you needed," I said, cupping her damp face and stroking her cheek with my thumb. "And I'd be the worst thing for you if I did."

Jen shook her head, looking down at her hands. Then she furiously pulled at the car door handle and was gone, whipping out of the passenger seat and taking the stairs to her Edwardian flat two at a time.

"Jen – " I called after her from the open passenger door, but she was inside the front door and slamming it before I could get another word out.

I made the slow drive to the hospital with a gaping hole in my middle, feeling as though my insides were being eaten away. Instantly, I missed her presence, like I'd left parts of myself on the pavement outside her flat. Coping without her would be agony, now that I knew what it was like to have her with me all the time.

A call came in as I drove. I answered on the hands-free system.

I was needed again in Royal London, and they needed to know if I could spare a few days. The patient I'd been due to assist with the day I saw Rebecca again had recovered enough to undergo anaesthetic.

"Gladly," I said, trying to hide the pain in my voice. This would at least provide me with a distraction, and keep me out of the lonely, silent apartment for long hours.

"You couldn't have asked at a better time."

I made my way to my office, where I would prepare to gather the team and explain that I was being called away, and that they'd have to manage without me. As I logged on to my computer, I heard the door go behind me. I swivelled in my chair, almost hoping against my better judgement that it was Jen, unable to keep away from me.

But my hopes were swiftly dashed when I saw Janine standing before me, holding a sealed envelope. My heart sank, realising what it was.

"My resignation," she said, passing the envelope to me. "I've given one already to my nursing administration, but I wanted you to see a copy of it too."

"Not full of vitriol about me, I hope?" I asked, taking the envelope.

Janine scoffed. "Get over yourself, Wes. It's time I moved on, did something new. See some new faces." She bowed her head, looking at her shoes.

I sighed, placing the letter down on my desktop. I stood, taking Janine by the shoulders. When she looked up, she had tears in her eyes.

"In spite of everything, you...will be very hard to replace, Janine," I said.

"I know," she said, smiling as a tear came loose and snaked down her cheek. "Tell me about it."

"I really need to thank you," I said, letting my hands fall to my sides. Janine looked confused, her brow furrowing.

"Thank me?"

"You've taught me a lot of things – some of them I've already mentioned. You made me realise how in love I was with Jennifer, and that I was over Rebecca for good – despite your real intention to sabotage us, of course."

Janine bowed her head again, having the decency to at least look sheepish about her meddling.

"But you also made me see something else – things about myself that I didn't know about. Things I didn't like. My self-centredness , my reluctance to change, wanting to keep everything convenient for myself...you were right about that."

"I was angry," said Janine.

"You were right."

Her eyes met mine, dark and shining.

"You spent years covering for my shortcomings, Janine. With my horrible temper, my inability to have the personal touch that every other nurse and doctor around here seems to have except me. And because of you, I'm stronger. I'm able to make selfless decisions now. Ones that might gut me inside – that destroy me and tear me up – but are best for the other person."

Janine frowned. "What are you talking about now?"

I pinched the bridge of my nose, knowing I wasn't being clear and was instead messing it all up. I sighed, resigning myself to never being able to really express just what Janine had done for me – especially knowing that Jen would likely not be so understanding of her.

"I'm trying to say thank you. That's all," I said, smiling briefly. "Wherever you end up – if you need a decent reference – you'll still be getting one from me."

"I earned it," said Janine, in her usual cocky and stubborn way – but before leaving, she shook my hand, and I felt we'd finally overcome something.

Then I was alone, determined not to cave in and contact Jen, even though my body was urging me to call her and bring her back to me at any cost.

Royal London would serve as a good distraction, but it was the time in between that I feared most – those moments when I would have a second to think of her, and instantly miss her. Those long evenings alone in bed without her, my body aching, in pain from the absence of her.

CHAPTER NINETEEN

Jennifer

A day off, and I was spending it curled up in my rumpled bed sheets that needed a wash about a month ago. My head thumped, still aching from the week's worth of crying and missing Wes so much that my core felt permanently empty.

My decision hadn't changed. I knew I would never see my parents again, and I would be deprived of my "birth right" – not that I cared a jot. But what hadn't improved was my understanding of why they'd hurt me so; why that ultimatum, uttered by my mother, had shattered my very soul.

I'd spent the week tormented, barely able to eat or sleep between shifts, and without Wesley to comfort me. So many moments had led me to his apartment building, where I failed at the last moment to approach the concierge at the front desk. I'd glanced up, the wind whipping my hair about my face as I struggled to see his penthouse, leaning back to see whether the light from his bedroom could be visible from the street.

And then I'd gone home, dejected, and curled up in my bed to cry.

It was a Saturday today. Summer was creeping lazily in. Birds chirped outside my fogged-up bedroom window, and I could see the leaves dancing on the branches of the trees outside my flat. Voices from my house mates drifted up the stairs; they were cooking something tasty for breakfast. Ordinarily I'd join then, but instead I gathered my duvet around my body and cocooned myself, wishing the world away.

The absence of Wes was driving me slowly mad.

I craved him, body and soul, and had to rock myself back and forth to sooth the aching. The void he left could never be filled, never be replaced.

And as I thought of him – how Wesley made me feel – it finally came to me.

I knew what I was grieving.

I sat up, throwing the duvet off and glancing out of my window to see the charming blue sky. Tears fell from my eyes, and I knew they were the last tears I'd ever cry for my parents.

Feeling sick without Wesley had given me clarity about why I was mourning my parents.

LIZA COLLINS

It was the absence of the relationship I'd *wanted* with them that was killing me; not the one I really had. I was grieving the fact that we would never repair and rebuild after this; that we would be marking the end, officially, of any pretence we'd kept up that there was love between me and my mum and dad.

I was grieving the loss of something that never existed. Something I'd been holding out hope for all my life – that I would have a healthy, loving, respectful relationship with my parents one day.

And finally, I had to accept that it was never going to happen.

Wiping my face, I called my mother's number and found myself going straight to voicemail. No matter, I thought – I could keep this short. As I made my way to the bathroom and turned on the shower, I waited for my opportunity to leave a message.

When it came, I cleared my throat, knowing this would be the last they'd ever hear from me.

"Mum, dad," I began, drawing in a deep breath. "I've made my decision."

♥

Panting from the exhaustion of running, I slowed as I entered the enormous atrium of Sacred Heart Children's Hospital; the one place, other than Wes' apartment – or his arms – where I felt truly at home.

I had failed to find him at his apartment or in the gym, and a call to the new charge nurse's desk had told me that his call-out to the Royal London had come to an end. That meant he had to be here, in this building. I was glad he'd been kept busy; the thought of him being in hell like I had been wasn't a pleasant one.

Though I hoped, of course, that he'd missed me.

As I scanned the atrium, a terrifying thought did briefly cross my mind. That he could have decided he didn't want me after all, and was happier going back to his old routine. That he could have decided he in fact did love Rebecca, and had already rekindled his relationship with her.

That I'd disappointed him, just like I'd disappointed my parents, and that he was disowning me entirely.

No, I told myself firmly. *He loves you. He did this for you. Now you need to find him.*

The hospital was incredibly busy for a weekend, with parents and buggies moving between the departments that branched off from the atrium. Knowing I hadn't a prayer of finding Wes in here, I made for the stairs leading down to the plastics department, hoping I might find him in his office.

As my hand touched the rail, my foot on the top step, a gentle tinkling of keys made me halt.

Among the bustle of the patients and families taking up the atrium, a gentle melody, just barely audible, filtered through the voices to me.

"I'm going crazy," I muttered, turning from the stairs and going towards the direction of the tune.

I found myself approaching the fountain I had come to love; the one of the little boy and girl crouching by the stream, with the water feature that soothed with its gentle trickling. I made my way around it, following the sound –

And saw Wes, standing at the piano, his head bowed in focus. His fingers were gently pressing the notes of *Moon River* into the keys.

His fingers paused, as if sensing me there, and he looked up. His emerald eyes glistened, seeing me, his mouth falling open as if to speak, and saying nothing.

I flew at him.

Throwing my arms around his neck, I hooked my legs around his waist and squeezed him, wishing I could climb inside his body and live there. I'd missed him so much that my core instantly became whole, my heart swelling as if with revitalised blood. I came alive again the moment my body met with his.

Wes squeezed me hard, muttering

gratitudes into the crook of my neck, before lowering me and drawing me into his embrace. I sank into his arms as he kissed me, deep and soft, while he cradled me against his chest.

With every fibre of his being, he told me – *welcome home.*

EPILOGUE

Jennifer

I waited for Wes outside the jewellers in Hatton Garden, my stomach gnawing and restless, ready for something to eat. Having spent hours and hours choosing bands and diamonds at our last appointment, my ring was finally ready.

My stomach was in knots with anticipation, knowing that the love of my life was inside, paying an eye-watering sum of money to buy me the perfect piece of jewellery. Our wedding – an intimate ceremony in a rooftop garden – was booked already. Now I just needed the ring to make things perfect. No longer would I be the fake fiancé, with a borrowed ring.

Wes found me outside as I was checking my new hairstyle in the reflection of the boutique store window. I'd chosen a sleek long bob, sophisticated and, best of all, the first haircut I'd ever chosen for myself. Gone was the schoolgirl ponytail.

Wes planted a soft kiss on my neck, stroking my hair as he gave me another on my crown.

"I didn't think you could get any more delectable, you know – but you've once again proven me wrong," he said.

I wound my arms around his waist and looked up at the eyes that had arrested me from the moment I first saw them. Smiling, I gently kissed the ridge of the scar on his lip, standing up on tip-toes. Wes closed his eyes and held me, enjoying the caress of my lips as I reminded him of my love for every imperfect part of him.

Then he opened them and, finding my hand, placed the cushioned ring box in my palm.

"Jesus, Wes – somebody might rob me for this!"

"Then you'd better put it on right now," he said, popping open the box and taking the ring in his thumb and forefinger.

He slid it gently onto my left ring finger and I beamed, holding it up to the light. The single solitaire dazzled, reflecting all the beauty of him – of us. The band fit snug and perfect, made to measure specifically for me.

As I laced my fingers with Wes', we walked hand in hand to the restaurant where we were meeting his parents. We would be showing them my new engagement ring – and doing a little explaining.

"Henrik and Oonagh deserve to know the truth," I said, as we planned what we would say. "I want to start properly, without any secrets, and build an honest relationship with them. They were so kind to me when they met me, when they could have been anything but."

Wes unlaced his hand from mine and wrapped his arm around my shoulders, squeezing me to him.

"Anyone would be proud to learn you're their prospective daughter-in-law," he said. "That's why we're about to tell them the good news."

"Again," I said. I held my hand out in front of me, admiring the shimmering diamond on my finger once more.

THE END

ABOUT THE AUTHOR

Liza Collins

Liza Collins is a wife and mother of two boys from the UK. She writes erotic romances to explore her fascination with assertive, intelligent, dashing heroes and the firecracker women who get their ties in a twist.

Visit www.LizaCollinsBooks.com to find out more.

BOOKS IN THIS SERIES

Sacred Heart Children's Hospital

The Nurse And The Neonatal Surgeon

The Intern And The Plastic Surgeon

The Intern And The Orthopaedic Surgeon

BOOKS BY THIS AUTHOR

The Nurse And The Neurosurgeon

The Suit And The Signorina

The Barrister And The Bridesmaid

The Mummy Maker

Made in United States
North Haven, CT
11 January 2025

64294094R00171